Finding Love on Cobble Wynd

Anne Hutchins

Copyright © 2021 Rachel Anne Hutchins

All rights reserved.

The characters, locations and events portrayed in this story are wholly the product of the author's imagination. Any similarity to any persons, whether living or dead, is purely coincidental.

ISBN: 9798720558697

Dedication

For my amazing Husband and our three Blessings
With All my Love xxx

Contents

The Town of Lillymouth	1
The Little Library on Cobble Wynd	3
A Bouquet of Blessings on Cobble Wynd	79
Love is the Best Medicine on Cobble Wynd	137
Epilogue	199
About the Author	203
Other Books in this Series	205

The Town of Lillymouth

In my books, the town of Lillymouth is situated at the easternmost point of the Lilly Valley, at the point where the river Lillywater meets the North Sea. Lillywater Bay benefits from its own harbour, enclosed by two piers, which is used daily by the local fishermen. Across the bay sits what is known locally as Smuggler's Rock.

Tracing its roots back to Roman times, it is said that a Roman lighthouse sat on the headland, in what was then known as Lighthouse Bay. The remains of this have long-since been pilfered for building purposes. Then, in 636 AD, a monastery stood on the hill behind what is now the town, with evidence of further dwellings from 1390. We pick up the story in 1910, during the reign of King Edward VII.

Enjoying a long beach and promenade, the town is favoured by holidaygoers in the summer season. Off the promenade is a well-landscaped park, with a bandstand and boating lake. There are two stone bridges which cross the Lillywater from the large town square, one leading to the train station, and the other to Bayview Farm and the surrounding countryside.

Also leading from the promenade, and to the town square and beyond, is a cobbled street known as Cobble Wynd. It is on the bottom corner of this lane that we find Bea's Book Nook, which you will hear about in the first story!

Cobble Wynd itself is a street of stalls and traders, leading up to the Church of Saint John the Evangelist, which takes prominent place at the top of the lane, along with the parish hall.

The Little Library on Cobble Wynd

ONE

Bea took a step back to admire her handiwork, careful not to tread in one of the many puddles which adorned the cobbled street. Her small shop window had been transformed. It had taken hours of work, and some improvisation on her part given Bea's very limited budget, but the display was welcoming and hopefully exciting for her young audience. Chalk-drawn animals framed the scene, and home-made bunting refashioned from an old tablecloth hung above. Below, a selection of toys sat at a teddy bear's picnic, apparently listening to *The Tale of Jemima Puddleduck* by Bea's namesake, Beatrix Potter. A few of the pieces had been Bea's own when she was little, and it warmed her heart to see them now in the window of her own bookshop. It was a childhood dream come true.

She ran her hands over her tattered floral apron, and pushed on the old wooden door to re-enter. The constant rain of the last few days was not helping the ancient, rusted hinges, and they squealed in protest as the door slowly budged. Opening day was tomorrow, and Bea hoped the weather would improve so as to entice families into the centre of their small, seaside town. Given her spot on the bottom corner of Cobble Wynd, Bea's shopfront had the benefit of being visible from both the promenade and the town square.

The room was still warm from the log fire which Bea had lit earlier, though now it was only glowing embers in the hearth. Standing her wet umbrella in the space at the bottom of the ornate bookstand by the door, Bea looked around her proudly at all she had achieved in the seven weeks since that fateful day in February when her life had changed in an instant…

Sitting in her freezing cold bedroom in the city, counting down until she had to begin her day working as a secretary in the office of Mr. Davies, a dour middle-aged chartered accountant, Bea had been surprised to hear the front doorbell chime far below her. Her landlady, the eccentric and elderly Mrs. Charters, had clearly not appreciated the interruption to her morning beauty routine, and had let the caller ring three times before answering. Bea's curiosity had been further piqued when she heard two sets of footsteps ascending to her attic room, before a portly, red-faced man, panting from the exertion of the six flights of stairs, was announced loudly by the retreating form of Mrs. Charters, still in her floral bedgown.

"A Mr. Michaels to see you, Beatrix! Though what he wants at this unearthly hour, goodness only knows!"

Bea smiled, as the clock on the landing chimed half past eight.

"Ah, Mr. Michaels, from Michaels, Russell and Groves," he held out a clammy palm which Bea reluctantly shook, as briefly as was possible whilst still being polite.

"My room is very small," Bea replied, suddenly self-conscious at the thought of having a man in her private space. Perhaps we could talk here on the landing?" She realised that the request was a bit odd, given that the space they occupied was no larger than four square feet, but Bea quietly closed her bedroom door and shuffled a couple of paces onto the landing.

"I'm not sure how I can help you, Mr. Michaels?" Bea

began hesitantly.

"Ah, my dear," he said, breathing more regularly now and smiling from ear to ear, "It is in fact I who can help you."

Bea was confused, but waited patiently as her visitor produced a manila file from his battered case.

"It pertains to the estate of your great uncle, one Barnabus Willoughby-Smythe."

"Uncle Banby? Well, he's my late father's uncle actually," Bea corrected herself, "but I haven't seen him since I was a child and we used to visit for our annual seaside holiday."

"Indeed, indeed," Mr. Michaels continued, rushing now to get to his point, "well, sadly, he passed away before Yuletide and that is where I come in!"

"Oh, I'm sorry to hear that," Bea responded, "though I'm still unsure as to …"

"Inheritance, my dear, inheritance is my business. And your uncle has left it all to you. Given that your parents are both passed, and you have no siblings, your great uncle himself having never had children either, you are the sole beneficiary of his entire estate."

Bea had retreated into her bedroom to steady herself as the news sunk in, whilst Mr. Michaels produced a pile of documents for her signature.

The inheritance, it transpired, was not in cash but rather a beautiful old shop and the rooms above, for which Bea now had complete ownership. She could have put it on the market of course, and taken the money, but Bea had remembered the musty smell of the books when she came to visit as a girl, the happiness of her parents, the shrieks of the seagulls outside the door, and the cosiness of the old place, and to be honest selling had not been an option for her. She had always been sentimental, but the nostalgia was too much for Bea to part with, she had so few remnants of her parents now.

Handing in her notice to the shocked Mr. Davies, who spluttered and coughed, but for once couldn't think of a stinging remark, pleased Bea greatly, as did paying her final rent cheque to Mrs. Charters. Bea had packed up her few belongings, bought a train ticket, and started her new life here.

Entering the shop for the first time hadn't exactly been the romanticised homecoming which Bea had imagined the whole way on her journey. Uncle Banby had never been fond of housekeeping, she remembered, but that had simply added to his charm. In his later years, however, he had clearly given up altogether and the clouds of dust assailed Bea as she pushed open the door on her new life. He must have sold the majority of his books to fund his retirement, living to the ripe old age of ninety-seven, as the shelves were mostly bare, bar a few scattered tomes, a lot of melted candle wax, several glass jars, ink bottles, and random sheets of yellowed paper. The old wingback chairs from Bea's memories remained at the back of the room, along with the coat stand, a mahogany side table with clawed feet and a china cabinet which contained an assortment of pinned bugs and butterflies from her uncle's lepidopterist hobby. The ancient cash register still stood proudly on the counter, and Bea had visions of playing with the keys when she was younger, hoisted up on her father's lap.

Upstairs had been even more of a shock, the roof having clearly developed a leak at some point. It had obviously been repaired, but the evidence still remained. Bea had used her last salary from her secretarial job to buy paints and decorating supplies, and soon the upstairs rooms were homely enough to be going along with – a far cry from her cold room in the attic, at least. Bea was surprised to see that her great uncle had installed a proper bathroom, a luxury to be sure. It was when Bea was trying to fix the plumbing on the neglected toilet in the bathroom, that she spotted a glint from behind the wooden panel in front of the bath. She had thought it odd that a stand-alone bath should have a wooden case, but given her uncle's eccentricity, Bea wasn't surprised. The panel had been roughly painted an off-white colour and she had assumed it hid damp, rot or some other such damage. Prying open the wooden frontage, Bea had been shocked to discover cash. Lots of it. Enough in fact to equip and stock her whole shop full of children's books, along with a cosy nook in the back corner, a tiny tearoom of sorts, where Bea planned to hold 'Rhyme and Chime' sessions during the day, and 'Read with Me' in the late afternoon on school days. She had been very frugal, keeping the old wooden shelves that went from floor to ceiling in the first half of the shop and simply sanding and varnishing them, but even then the money only stretched so far. Bea had retained a small portion to see her through her first six months of trading, until her shop became established, but the pot was small and she needed to keep watching every penny.

She had made it through, however, and tomorrow was her grand opening! Bea looked around the interior of the bookshop at all she had achieved. Books for babies and toddlers in a train-shaped, low level bookcase at the far end, near the armchairs for their carers to have conversation and refreshments. Then books for primary aged children, with some wooden games and toys scattered throughout. Finally, the section for more advanced readers closest to the door, where the independent youths could spend time away from the adults, and where a selection of non-fiction works were housed. It wasn't perfect, more a work in progress, but Bea breathed a happy sigh as she sat down behind the ancient cash register, one relic she'd decided to keep as a talking point for the children, and surveyed her little sanctuary, wondering what tomorrow would bring.

Two

"Daddy, Daddy!" Liv pulled on her father's hand and tried to drag him towards the new shop she had spotted on the corner.

"Have patience, Livvy!" Aaron skidded on the wet cobbles as he was yanked along by his daughter, who was apparently very strong for a seven year old.

Clearly, he saw, she had set her sights on the new children's book shop which they had seen being prepared the previous week. They only came into town once a week, on a Friday afternoon, as Aaron schooled Liv at home every day in their small caravan on the hill outside of town. At first, she had complained that she couldn't join the other youngsters skipping down the hill with their parents to the small primary school in the centre, but now she simply accepted their routine mutely. She understood, he hoped, that he was simply trying to keep her safe.

"Be-a's Book Nook," Liv spelled out the shop sign as they neared the doorway.

"I think it's pronounced, 'Bee' as in 'tea', sweetheart," Aaron helped her gently, "not 'beya' like 'Freya.'"

"Oh, well anyhow, can we go inside Daddy? Look, look at the toys in the window!"

Aaron hesitated. He didn't want to say no, but at the same time he knew that he couldn't afford a new book and he didn't want to court his daughter's disappointment. The freelance bookkeeping which he did in the evenings for a few local businesses hardly managed to pay the bills as it was. When combined with a quickly-growing girl and an ancient wooden home that was in need of constant repairs, every single penny was spent in keeping their small ship afloat. Nevertheless, they both peered through the open door curiously, outside of which a blackboard had been positioned, reading 'Please do pop in to say hello!' with a big hand-drawn smiling face in white chalk.

Bea sat on a stool behind the counter twiddling her

thumbs. She was starting to regret not having her Grand Opening on Saturday, but had hoped to attract the crowd of schoolchildren and their parents excited to be going home for the weekend. A few had poked their heads in to have a quick look, but none had stayed for the free tea and cake she was offering. Bea sighed, almost ready to give up for the day and start again tomorrow, when she spotted the two heads peeking in.

Shooting up from her spot and rushing over, smoothing her apron as she walked, Bea extended a hand to the young girl, "Hello, I'm Bea!" she said, bending to make eye contact with the child.

"I know, your name is up there!" Liv giggled, pointing to the sign.

"Liv!" Aaron chided his daughter's rudeness and she immediately took Bea's hand, saying,

"Sorry, Miss Bea, I'm Liv and this is my father, Aaron."

"A pleasure to meet you, it's Aaron McBain" Aaron said, extending his hand to Bea in turn and shaking hers gently.

"Will you come in? Have a look around?" Bea asked, stepping to the side and gesturing for them to enter.

"I, ah, we really must be…" Aaron stuttered.

"I have tea and cake to celebrate my not-so-grand opening," Bea added ruefully.

"Please, Daddy, cake, please!" Liv shouted, unable to dampen her exuberance.

"Oh, okay then," Aaron capitulated, running his fingers over the few coins in his pocket.

"Please…" Bea showed the way and the pair followed. Liv was soon lost to her own explorations, the promise of cake forgotten as she ooh'd and ahh'd over the books and toys, whilst the adults made their way to the seating area at the back of the shop.

Aaron took an awkward seat on one of the cosy chairs, perching on the edge as if ready to take flight, "Ah, nothing for me, please, thank you," he stammered, as he saw Bea busy preparing two cups of tea and a cup of milk for Liv, beside a plate of small, home-made cherry cakes.

"Really?" Bea turned and smiled, though inwardly contemplating his rather unkempt appearance – a large hole in his cardigan was only slightly hidden by the well-worn blazer, and his trousers appeared frayed at the hems. Bea did not judge. It was not in her nature, besides she had known enough poverty in her own life to understand that keeping your pride and dignity was more important than anything. So she simply said, "I'm afraid if you don't help me eat these, they will go to waste! I laid on a bit of a treat for my first customers, and no-one decided to take me up on the offer!" She felt herself blush at her own honesty, but was happy when the man before her visibly relaxed.

"Oh, in that case, it would be rude to refuse!" Aaron replied, rubbing his face and pushing his floppy hair back from his eyes. He had a boyish charm about him, which Bea found endearing. He reminded her a little of the younger version of Uncle Banby, or at least how she imagined him to have been – gangly and tall, but with an innate chivalry and sense of fun about him.

"How do you take your tea?" Bea asked, surprised at the happiness she felt at simply having an adult to converse with. Apart from running errands to the other shops on Cobble Wynd and a few quick chats here and there with curious townsfolk, she had mainly kept herself to herself since arriving here, her weekly visits to church the only exception.

"Oh, white no sugar, please," Aaron replied distractedly, eyeing Liv who was amassing quite a pile of books where she stood at the shelves.

"Perfect," Bea passed him a china cup and saucer, before arranging the plate of cakes on the table between them and taking a seat herself, blowing the steam from her cup. Seeing the subject of his gaze, she thought for a moment before adding, "Of course, there is a free book for every child, too, to celebrate opening day."

"Really?" Aaron turned to face her, his expression slightly sceptical.

"Of course, the children are my customers, I must keep them happy!" Bea said lightly, standing to fetch the milk as Liv came to join them.

"Look Daddy, look! I've narrowed it down to these five!"

"That's great, sweetpea, why don't you have a drink and some cake," Aaron urged his daughter onto a wooden stool and placed the pile of books to the other side of him.

"I could read you the first few pages of one of those, if you like," Bea offered, then if you enjoy it you can choose that one – the others will still be here next time!"

"Ooh, yes please," Liv responded excitedly, jumping

up and sifting through the pile once more. Aaron sat back and let the two females discuss each book, sipping his tea and grateful for the warmth of the open fire. As a decision was finally made, and Bea began to read from Beatrix Potter's *The Tale of Mrs Tiggy-Winkle,* Aaron felt himself lulled by the almost musical voice of the young woman opposite. He guessed she was maybe a couple of years younger than him, though he often felt much older than his own age of twenty-eight, a fact not helped by sleeping in a chair every night. Dressed modestly in an ivory coloured blouse and ankle-length tweed skirt, she looked quite adorable in her apron and reading spectacles. Feeling his eyelids become heavy, Aaron placed his cup and saucer on the table and dozed off to the sound of her melodic voice.

THREE

Bea smiled to herself as she heard the small snores of the man opposite her, and kept reading further than she'd originally intended. Liv seemed engrossed, and if her father's dark shadows under his eyes were anything to go by, he was not used to getting much sleep. *This is the least I can do*, Bea thought to herself, enjoying the story which was one of her own favourites amongst the new stock. She encouraged Liv to eat the cakes, hoping to fill her up a little, and paused to refill her cup of milk.

"Please may we have a break, now?" Liv asked when her fourth cake was finished, "so that I may look at the toys?"

"Of course," Bea smiled at her, noticing that the girl, too, looked like she needed a good night's sleep.

At the stirring and scraping of his daughter's stool, Aaron awoke with a jolt. Suddenly embarrassed, he shot up and knocked over the now-cold remains of his drink, sloshing them over the table. Thankfully, the cup was not chipped and he handed it to Bea apologetically, "I am so sorry, please let me clear this up."

"Not at all, it is merely a few drops, soon remedied!" Bea took a dishcloth from beside the small sink and wiped the table down.

"You must think me so rude," Aaron continued, "for, ah, dozing off." He felt his cheeks flame red beneath his freckles and turned away, "Come, Livvy, we must be getting back!"

"Oh Daddy, I was just…"

"Now, Elizabeth!" His tone brooked no argument, and Liv knew better that to try, so she returned to Bea, who was now wrapping the book in brown paper at the main counter, a small lollipop nestled in the string which she tied around the parcel.

"Thank you, Miss Bea," she said politely.

"You are most welcome, Liv," Bea smiled at the girl's manners, before addressing her father, "It was such a pleasure to meet you both. I hope you won't be strangers to my little shop."

"Of course not!" Liv chimed in before her father could respond, "We will visit every Friday when we're in town!"

"I, well, I mean, I… it was a pleasure," Aaron stuttered before guiding his daughter out of the shop with a palm placed on her back, as Bea waved them goodbye, a small frown marring her pretty features.

Returning through the drizzle to the old caravan on the hill, its gaudy paintwork long-since faded, and placing the small, netted bag of groceries on the tiny table, Aaron sighed as he took in their surroundings. Not for the first time that week, he berated himself for his lack of provision – this was no place to raise a child, especially one that would soon be nearing womanhood. Frustrated at his lack of options, he encouraged Liv to get ready for bed, before making some toast on the small stove.

"But Daddy, it is not late," she whined.

"You know I have my daily work still to begin," Aaron tried to keep the annoyance and tiredness from his voice, but clearly failed as Liv began crying, silent tears, which she tried to hide by walking into her tiny bedroom cupboard. "Ah, come here, love," he followed her and held her tightly when she turned to embrace him. "Ignore your grumpy old papa, I'm just tired. Let's eat together, and then we can read some of that delightful new book!" Liv wiped her watery eyes and sat at the table.

Aaron felt his guilt at upsetting her coil like a snake within him, taking away what little appetite he had. *Perhaps she would have been better with her grandmother*, he wondered silently, though knowing deep down that he would never have let that happen. When his wife had left them, when Liv was only six months old, having argued for months that she had never been maternal, no longer loved him, found their life together suffocating and wanted the freedom to travel and explore, Aaron had not been given the option to try to stop her. It would have been for naught, anyway, as Gwen had always been confident and headstrong in nature, the complete opposite to him, in fact. It had come as a shock to Aaron when she had accepted his proposal in the first place. He had assumed that, whilst he had fallen for her hard, to her he was just a plaything until the right match was found. Coming from a wealthy, titled family, Gwen had been expected to marry a similar landowner or heir, not the trainee from the accountancy firm used by her father. Then again, he had always wondered, in the part of his heart that dared not form the words, whether she had used her marriage as a way to both anger her family and to escape the tight control which they held over her life. Certainly, she had taken much pleasure in her rebellion.

For the few years of their doomed marriage, they had lived in a small cottage on her father's estate, close enough for her meddling grandmother to keep a hawk's eye on them. Gwen had hidden neither her disappointment in Aaron nor in their lack of funds – all resources still coming from her allowance. She railed at his inability to provide, and snook out regularly, presumably to meet those who could give her what she sought. It was when Gwen became pregnant, however, that the real arguments began. She told Aaron that she herself had never wanted to be a mother, her own mother having died in Gwen's youth from a sudden illness. Nor did she wish to be tied down by a family. Thus, when their baby was only six months old, she simply did not return from one of her night-time flits. No note, no message. When a month had gone by, and still nothing was heard, Gwen's grandmother, the unassailable Lady Harris, had stopped by to tell him that Liv would now live with her and Aaron was to leave the cottage, the estate and the town forthwith, forgetting he ever had a wife or child.

Of course, Aaron could not allow this, so he had packed the few things that did not come from family money, cradled his child to him, and used what tiny earnings he had to buy a train ticket south, to a random town on the map that he hoped Gwen's family had never heard of. In the seven years since they'd lived in the once-horse-drawn home, Aaron had not heard a peep from the Harris family – neither Gwen nor her relations – and glad he was of it, for if they ever did find Liv's whereabouts he would be forced to run with his daughter once again.

FOUR

That weekend the sun shone down, the days were graced with only a few April showers, and a few holidaymakers descended on the seaside town. Bea felt the benefit of both the good weather, and her shop's position near the promenade, as she had a steady stream of customers eager for both teas and entertainment for their children. A few books and wooden games were sold, cake crumbs were scattered everywhere from little people eager to get back to choosing, and the old cash register provided a great talking point for young and old alike. All in all, Bea considered her first Saturday a success.

As Sunday was a day of rest, Bea rose early for the first

church service, so that she would have the rest of the day to explore the blossoming Spring season in her local area. Packing a light lunch, putting on her old walking boots, and bringing a warm shawl, she set off just before lunchtime, happy to be out in the fresh air for a while. After meandering along the beach and taking a stroll through the local park, where she stopped in the bandstand to have her sandwiches, Bea decided to make the small trek up the hill which overlooked the centre of their small town. She had heard that there was a grand tearoom in a hotel overlooking the bay, which served the best afternoon teas. She wasn't going to try them out today, but hoped to in the summertime when business had picked up more. Anyway, it wouldn't hurt to see the views from up there too, as Bea couldn't remember them from her visits as a child.

The stony path which edged the single track road was steep and Bea had to pause to catch her breath at the top. Hunched over as she was, she heard only the shouted, "Miss Bea!" first, without seeing the voice's owner. Peering over the small hedge into the field beyond, Bea spotted the red curls of Liv, bouncing on her shoulders as she ran towards her.

"Miss Bea! It's me!" the girl shouted as she closed the distance between them, throwing her skipping rope to the side on the grass and stopping directly opposite Bea on the other side of the hedge.

"Hello, Liv!" Bea smiled, scanning behind the youngster for signs of her father, wondering why she was this far out of town apparently alone, "Is your dad here?"

"Yes – well, he's not here, he's mending the wagon roof again, over there!" Liv pointed behind her to the other side of the field, where behind a copse of trees Bea caught a glimpse of colour.

"Ah," Bea nodded, still not sure whose caravan Aaron would be mending, having thought she recalled him telling her he was an accountant.

"Come with me!" Liv hopped up and down excitedly, "we don't get visitors, he'll be so happy to see you!"

"Well, I..." Bea wasn't so sure, she didn't want to disturb a man she barely knew, at work. Yet, Liv had hold of her hand over the hedge and was guiding her to the gate a few yards further down the track. The girl's enthusiasm was contagious, and Bea decided it could do no harm to just say hello quickly and then take her leave.

"Daddy!" Liv's shouts heralded their arrival, and Aaron looked down from his precarious spot atop the wooden ladder, expecting his daughter to have found a daisy or some such childish delight. To his horror, he saw that she had found something much more beautiful – the kind lady from the bookshop. Wobbling, he had to grab the top of the caravan to steady himself, before slowly descending, a feeling of dread filling his gut. *How would he explain their home? The state of it?* He could already feel his cheeks flaming in embarrassment. There was nothing for it, but to be rude to the woman and send her on her way.

"Good afternoon, Mr. McBain," Bea smiled at the man stepping off the ladder.

"Miss Willoughby-Smythe," Aaron replied tersely, nodding in acknowledgement before turning his back on her and heading straight inside to wash his hands.

"Daddy, it's the lady from the shop!" Liv scolded in a stage whisper.

"It's okay, sweet, your daddy is clearly very busy," Bea tried to placate the child, "I'm sure I'll see you in town soon."

"No! Don't go!" Liv shouted, clinging onto Bea's arm and looking pleadingly towards the doorway of their little home.

Aaron heard their exchange and felt further shame. *How could I not even provide a place suitable for guests?* He balled his hands into fists in the ragged towel he was using and tried to take a few calming breaths before exiting the dilapidated wagon again. "Miss…ah, Bea, please accept my apology for my blunt welcome. I'm afraid you caught me fixing our roof. How are you today?" he asked, trying to force a smile.

Bea did not let her expression change in the slightest, though inside she registered a small shock at his admission that this was their home. Not of judgement, but of sympathy. She could only imagine how he was feeling right now. Probably similar to how she had felt when the other secretaries wanted to come back to her attic room for a drink – she had always found excuses to appease their curiosity.

"I am very well, Aaron, just taking a Sunday stroll. My apologies for disturbing you at your task," Bea smiled to try and put the man at ease. His hands were shoved in the pockets of his faded trousers and he hung his head as if in defeat. Her heart went out to him. "Perhaps you and Liv would like to join me?" she suggested, keen that he not feel obliged to invite her in.

"Can we, Daddy?"

"Yes, sweetpea," he replied to his daughter, before looking directly at Bea for the first time that day. Relief and gratitude were etched into his taut features. "That would be lovely, Bea, thank you, a break is just what I need!"

"Perfect," Bea replied, opening her small, quilted bag and taking out an apple which she held out in offering to Liv. The girl took the fruit joyfully, running off to fetch her discarded skipping ropes to use on their walk.

They set off across the field in which the caravan stood, Aaron explaining that the land belonged to a farmer, whose accounts he did in return for use of the caravan. "He will not mind us walking across here," he added, smiling at Bea, "there is a duckpond on the other side of the farmhouse which Liv and I sometimes visit."

"That sounds perfect," Bea smiled and then quickly looked away as the heat in his blue eyes made her stomach do a funny little flip. *Very unsettling*, she decided, and wondered if the sardines in her sandwiches may not have been a bit off.

They chatted about the local area, Liv's enjoyment of nature and their shared love of books, whilst Bea brought the remnants of her half-eaten sandwiches out of her bag for Liv to feed the ducks and swans. The girl seemed to be in her element, and Bea noticed that Aaron, too, had finally relaxed. He was guarded about their life before the caravan, and Bea gathered it was not wise to press him for information, so she talked about how she had come into her inheritance, about childhood holidays, and Uncle Banby. Aaron had laughed at the stories of her uncle's antics – which had always made his nephew, Bea's father, shake his head ruefully – and Bea loved the deep timbre of the sound. It also further intensified the strange flutterings within. Worried that she may make a fool of herself by fainting, as surely this must be a food poisoning or illness of some sort, Bea sat on the grass and fanned herself with her cotton bag.

"Are you okay, Bea?" Aaron enquired, clearly concerned, "You appear slightly flushed."

"I am fine, thank you for your concern," Bea felt her face heat further under his scrutiny and changed the subject back to Liv instead.

When the afternoon air began to chill their bare arms, Aaron and Liv walked Bea back to the main path and they took their leave. Bea had made them promise to visit her in the shop on Friday, for more tea and cake. Her treat, she assured them, for being such lovely company today. Liv squealed delightedly at the offer, and Aaron agreed, though Bea sensed his slight reluctance. Plans made, they said goodbye, and Bea made her way back down the hill, with much food for thought on which to ponder.

FIVE

The week passed much more slowly that Bea would have liked. She had placed flyers advertising her toddler sessions and after-school book group in the parish hall, on the school noticeboard, in the florist's and grocer's windows, but she knew it would take time for word to get around. Nevertheless, she had two well-to-do mothers with their babes on Friday morning for a rhythm and bounce baby class, which thankfully made the day go faster. Bea couldn't understand why her stomach felt so fluttery or her concentration was so limited. Of course, she knew deep down that it more than likely had to do with her impending visitors, but she would not admit to herself that it might be more than that.

At the grand old age of twenty-five, Bea had experienced feelings for members of the opposite gender before, of course, but nothing that had ever progressed beyond that – feelings. She had found an unmarried associate of Mr. Davies particularly handsome, and had even chatted with him during tea breaks, but had never felt the courage to give him any sign of her growing affection. Even when she had caught him looking at her intently on several occasions, Bea had resisted the desire to be more obvious. And so here she was. A spinster and firmly on the shelf. Shaking her head to rouse herself from pointless thoughts, Bea began brewing the tea and cutting the cake for Liv and Aaron. It was just exciting to have made a friend. That was all. Nothing more to it.

When the bell over the door chimed to announce their arrival, it was half past three and Bea smiled as she rose from her place on the floor, where she had been tidying the lower bookshelves.

"Bea!" Liv greeted her with an enthusiastic embrace, and immediately picked up a small ragdoll which sat on the shelf nearby.

"Hello, Bea," Aaron smiled and offered his hand which Bea shook distractedly, noticing that he had greased his hair into place and had a shave. Struck by how much more handsome even that small change made him, Bea said a hasty good afternoon, before rushing to the tea nook, embarrassed that he may have noticed her clammy hand and pink cheeks. She need not have worried, however, as Aaron took his same seat as before and they chatted easily whilst Liv ran between them and the bookshelves, grabbing bites of cake as she went. Bea stood a few times to chat with other customers, and told Aaron he must stay when he offered for them to leave, so five o'clock found all three still in the shop.

"Well, we really must be making tracks," Aaron began, picking up the small bag of groceries which lay at his feet.

"Which book can I have this week, Daddy?" Liv asked, carrying the ragdoll, which she had named Rose, over along with a stack of books.

"I, ah well," Aaron stuttered, looking at his daughter with the eyes of a parent trying silently to communicate their displeasure. Liv chose not to notice her father's expression, and instead looked hopefully at Bea who hovered uncomfortably beside them.

Desperate to avoid a scene which would embarrass Aaron, as she had guessed that he could not afford his daughter's request, Bea was struck with an idea.

"Well," she said, crouching to look at Liv, "I've been thinking this week. "When I was a girl your age, one of my favourite games was to pretend to be a librarian. I would have my few toys and a couple of books and pretend to stamp them with a date on a card inside, so that my clothes-peg dolls would know when they should return them!" Liv giggled at the notion. Bea caught Aaron's eye as he looked down at the pair, and the gratitude she saw there put a lump in her throat. Swallowing it back down, she continued quickly, "So, ah, I thought I could make a little library shelf here. Where children could borrow a book, then return it to exchange for another the next week."

"Bea," Aaron interrupted gruffly, his own throat having become somewhat scratchy, "your beautiful new books will become worn and damaged."

"I'm sure the children will take good care of them," Bea replied, her mind made up, "You will, Liv, won't you?"

"Yes!" Liv cried happily.

"Well then, you can help me choose ten books to start the little library, and Miss Rose the Ragdoll here can be the librarian! She can come home with you to help you look after the book!"

"Really, Bea, it's too kind…" Aaron interjected awkwardly.

"Nonsense, as I say it is a plan that has been brewing for quite some time!" Bea turned her back to hide the white lie from her face, and began chatting with Liv about a selection of books that would attract all boys and girls to the library. When the task was complete, and Liv and Rose had made this week's choice, Bea stuck a small envelope inside the front cover of the book. Into this, she placed a rectangular piece of pale blue cardboard on which she wrote the following Friday's date. The look of joy and pleasure on the girl's face was enough payment for Bea for a dozen library books.

"I can't thank you enough," Aaron whispered to her as they followed Liv out of the shop, the youngster chatting happily to her doll and clutching the precious book to her chest.

The feel of his breath on her cheek when he leaned in to her to speak, the smell of him, sent Bea's senses whirling and she hastily said her goodbyes, waving them off as they began the long walk home.

SIX

As they entered May that following week, and the weather improved considerably, the little town began to come to life. There was a new bustle and business about the place, the shop had a steady stream of customers – some for the tea nook and chatter, others for the books and games. Before she had a chance to catch her breath, Bea realised that it was Friday. As she put on her best summer dress that morning, Bea chided herself for making an extra effort. Telling herself that it was just in honour of the beautiful sunshine they'd been having, and knowing fine well that was another white lie, Bea hurried down to open the shop. At lunchtime, she closed up for half an hour to rush back upstairs. She didn't normally take a lunch break, just ate something light in the shop, but today she wanted to put a cake batter in the oven. Marble cake, which Aaron may have mentioned was his favourite when she asked him last week!

At half past three on the dot the bell chimed and Bea found herself blushing like a lovesick schoolgirl at the sight of him, his shirt sleeves rolled up to expose well-toned arms, and him smiling back at her as if he, too, had been anticipating this visit all week long.

"Miss Bea, I remembered them!" Liv said proudly, breaking the magic between the couple.

Bea didn't mind, she looked forward to seeing the girl too, and reached out to embrace her, before taking the book which was ceremoniously offered.

"See, I kept it in beautiful condition!" Liv placed the book reverently on the counter and took Rose to look at the library shelf, which had now grown to about thirty books.

"I lent some to three other children this week," Bea smiled down at her, "I think word may be starting to get round, as the last young lad told me that he'd heard from his friend at school about my little library!" Finishing her sentence, Bea noticed that Aaron had begun making the hot drinks. The sight of him doing something so homely in her space sent a warmth running through Bea that she couldn't deny. To distract herself from that unsettling thought, she went behind the old wooden counter and picked up the book, making a show of crossing out the date for Liv to see, indicating that it had been returned. When she pulled the piece of card out of the envelope to do so, however, Bea felt something else inside. Pulling gently, she discovered it was a piece of paper, folded so many times so as to make it tiny and almost invisible. Surprised, Bea took the mini package and placed it in her apron pocket, looking in Aaron's direction as she did so to find him staring at her nervously. It struck Bea suddenly, that perhaps the hidden message may not be from Liv, so she kept her mouth shut on the subject and said simply, "I'm so ready for a hot drink! And I have a marble cake in the cupboard!"

Their conversation flowed easily again, and Bea chatted happily about her work, eager to hear Aaron's news too. Whilst he was guarded about his background, he was more than happy to share snippets of information about his local clients, about Bayview Farm where he lived and about his hopes for the future. They included Liv in their discussion, too, and she talked about the birds she had seen and the shells she loved to find on the beach. All the while, Bea was aware of the tiny paper bundle in her pocket, as if it were a precious gem to be protected and cherished. Bea had thought during the week, how lovely it would be to invite the pair to supper one Friday. They could stay until the shop closed at half past five and then come upstairs to eat. Now that the moment had come to make the invitation, however, Bea found herself procrastinating the offer, to the point that she managed to talk herself out of it entirely.

When another Rose-approved library book had been chosen, the cake enjoyed and the remainder packed in rice paper for them to take home, Bea waved the pair off again, sad that their Friday visit was over for another week. She still had the piece of paper, though, she could not have forgotten that, and rushed inside, locking the heavy door behind her and changing the shop sign to Closed. Eagerly, Bea fished the little parcel out of her apron and unfolded it carefully. Inside, in smudged black ink, it read,

Dear Bea,

I cannot thank you enough for what you have done for Livvy, and for me. To give her a new book to borrow and to read every week, is such a special gift. Moreover, your generosity in welcoming us to your shop each Friday, refusing to take payment for the refreshments, along with your heartily good company... well, it is the highlight of my week. Please know that you are appreciated beyond measure.

Your friend,

Aaron

Bea read the note through several times, savouring the message inside and the feel of the paper between her fingers. The fact that he had taken the time to write, as well as his words inside the note, meant more to Bea than she could explain, even to herself. She felt her eyes welling with tears, emotional all of a sudden to have made such a connection. Without hesitation, she brought out her own pen and ink pot and wrote a reply, which she intended to pop into next week's book,

Dear Aaron,

Thank you so much for your kind note. You and Liv are welcome here any time, and as my friends of course the tea and cakes are complimentary! It is my pleasure to share them with you! I am loving that the children are enjoying my little library, and I intend to continue it, expanding my range even.

I look forward to your company and conversation so much, and I am always sad to see you both leave. On

that note, perhaps you and Liv would like to have supper with me one Friday evening?

Your friend always,

Bea

And so the messages began, always hidden in the books which Liv borrowed, always more reserved than either would have wished. Sharing a secret between them, however innocent it was, gave Bea the feeling of having a special bond with Aaron, and he with her, so that when they saw each other they began to lower their natural barriers. A quick peck on the cheek when they met, eyes meeting across the room in mutual understanding, a small touch of fingers when the hot drinks were handed across. All of these small touches Bea treasured within her, scared to speak aloud her feelings lest she scared him away, and frightened that the unspoken gestures they shared would end.

SEVEN

It was a beautiful summer's evening in early July, when the trio were sharing a Friday evening picnic on the beach. Bea had laid out a blanket on the sand, Liv was hunting for shells, and Aaron had removed his shoes and socks, rolled up his trousers, and been for a paddle in the sea. The water was freezing, yet he eventually managed to persuade Bea to remove her shoes and join him for a dip up to her ankles. Bea shrieked as a cold wave hit her and jumped away from it giggling, landing unexpectedly with her back against Aaron. Turning slowly to apologise, she found they were standing close to one another – much closer than propriety allowed. Yet neither of them moved. They simply stared into each other's eyes, seemingly mesmerized.

Bea felt as if time itself stood still. The shrieks of the children playing in the sand around them, and the seagulls adding their chorus overhead, died down somehow, and she was aware only of the tall man in front of her. When he bent slowly, until their faces were a mere hairsbreadth apart, then raised his hand to cup her cheek, Bea felt herself go weak at the knees. She wondered if he were about to kiss her, wanted him to, panicked that he might and then...

"Daddy!" The sound of Liv's voice caused them to jump apart abruptly, as if they had been caught doing something illicit. "Daddy! Look at this shell the kind lady found for me!"

Aaron looked beyond his daughter to the older woman behind her. Dressed all in black, with a hat that sported a lavish raven's feather, stood his absent wife's grandmother, Lady Harris, in all her disdainful glory. Rushing forward, he physically lifted Liv and placed her behind him.

Seeing Aaron blanch and rush to his daughter, Bea knew immediately that something was amiss. Worryingly so. She held Liv's hand tightly and acted as if to admire the shell, whilst keeping an eye on Aaron and the elderly woman. She could tell from his hand gesticulations that he was agitated.

"Well, she wants to speak with me, don't you dear?" the woman remarked loudly, pushing past Aaron and advancing on Liv.

"I, ah…" Liv did not want to anger her father further.

"I don't think we've met," Bea spoke up, stepping forward to stand between the girl and the older lady, "Miss Beatrix Willoughby-Smythe."

Apparently impressed by the grandiose-sounding name, Lady Harris returned Bea's introduction with a nod and her name, before adding, "And who are you in relation?"

Bea stood silent a moment, not sure who she really was to Aaron and his daughter. Friend? Confidante? More?

"Well, dear, has the cat got your tongue?"

"Miss Bea owns the bookshop and little library," Liv answered for her, unsure why the grown-ups were acting so oddly all of a sudden.

"And we must be getting back," Aaron took Liv's hand and started dragging her away, the picnic things, and Bea herself, apparently forgotten.

"Well, you can't be anything important to him," the

old woman eyed Bea sourly and with a calculating look added, "as he is already married to my granddaughter!"

Bea could not have been more shocked. She stood, open-mouthed, as she was left alone on the beach. Lady Harris walked on with her small entourage of servants, casting not a single backward glance, and Bea tried to swallow down her heart, which all of a sudden felt lodged in her throat.

Trying to hide the tears, which streamed with wanton abandon down her face, from the worried glances of the other beachgoers, Bea knelt and tidied their few picnic items. She picked up Aaron's footwear and Liv's shoes, adding those to the hamper too, before struggling to lift it and making her way slowly back along the beach in the direction of the town square.

Whilst her sobs had been silent, once she was back in the sanctuary of her little shop, the door bolted behind her, Bea dropped to her knees and let the torrent of emotions flood her. She could hold her composure no longer. Months of hiding her love for the man who had taken root in her heart, only to end in the knowledge that he had misled her. Or worse, had deliberately strung her along, knowing that he was already attached to another. It was almost too much to bear. Her chest heaved and ached, and Bea could hardly get her head around the events of the past hour. The words of the woman in black whirled around ominously in all her thoughts, combined with pictures of Aaron – his smiling blue eyes, his floppy blond hair, his hearty laugh – and of Liv's little face beaming up at her. To have them wrenched from her so suddenly left an ache so grand that Bea didn't know how she would ever recover.

Bea woke a while later, slumped against the counter, her hair plastered to her still-damp face and with a headache that she imagined could match any regular imbiber. Glancing to the window she saw that darkness had now fallen. Chilled, Bea struggled to her feet, her legs and back protesting at the position she'd been in. Given the season, there was no warming fire in the grate and she moved to pull the blinds so that she could disappear upstairs to her bed. Lowering the blind on the glass of the main door, Bea shrieked when a figure emerged quickly from the shadows, hammering on the door on the other side of which she stood, as if their life itself depended on it.

Raising the thin linen cautiously, Bea was shocked to see Aaron staring back at her, little Liv huddled to his side, half hidden under his coat. He held two suitcases and had a wild air about him that scared her, yet Bea unbolted the door to allow them entry. *What else could she do?* Her head told her that this would only lead to more pain, but her heart lurched to see them standing there when she had thought to never set eyes on them again.

EIGHT

"Bea," Her name on his tongue as he rushed inside, pushing Liv ahead of him, caused Bea to shuffle backwards as they entered. The feeling it provoked was akin to a smack in the face, and she couldn't bear the thought there might be any physical contact between them, struggling as she already was to hold her emotions in check.

"Hello, Livvy sweetling, are you okay?" Bea knelt beside the shivering child, seeing her tear-streaked face and that she was clutching Rose to her.

"Oh, Miss Bea," Liv's sobs began anew and she buried her head against Bea's shoulder, hiccoughing and spewing a torrent of words, out of which Bea could only catch a few.

Bea put her arms around the girl and rubbed her back gently. "There, there, let's go upstairs and make some hot milk, then we'll get you ensconced and warm in my bed." Bea had no idea if that was the correct thing to say or do, but it was clearly what the child needed. She looked up to see Aaron's face, gaunt in the moonlit room, frowning down at her, but he said nothing to contradict her plan.

So the three of them trudged upstairs to the small apartment, where Bea set some milk to heat on the stove, and Aaron fished in a case for the girl's nightwear. Seeing her cosied up in bed with her ragdoll, a warm drink and a biscuit, Bea returned to the sitting room where Aaron was laying a fire in the grate. She took a seat in the wing-backed chair by the hearth, indicating that he should take the other, and then Bea waited, silently, for him to explain.

Aaron rubbed his hands together distractedly, looking everywhere but at Bea. Tempted as she was to question him, she held her tongue until the silence became unbearable and he finally began talking.

"I'm sorry Bea, so sorry." He whispered, so that Bea had to lean forwards to hear him. In the small space between the chairs, their knees were almost touching and she felt the waves of his sorrow, desperate to reach out to him, but forcing her hands to remain as still as her voice.

"I should be on the road now, with Livvy, we need to get away, you see… No, you probably don't see," he paused and studied her intently before continuing, "we can't be in town when that woman comes back. She probably already knows where we live. She has contacts. Though why it's taken her seven years…" He trailed off, lost in his own thoughts.

Bea could remain silent no longer. "Start at the beginning," she said quietly, "for until you do, I can make no sense of the matter."

Aaron sighed heavily and ran his fingers through his hair. Bea lifted his untouched cup of tea from the side table and handed it to him, his shaking hands making the cup clatter against the saucer as he took it from her. "Here, drink this," she encouraged, "take a moment before you begin, to calm your mind."

Aaron quirked his mouth in gratitude. It was not a smile, not even close, but Bea was thankful to see a hint of his normal good humour returning. Lowering the now half-full cup slowly to its doily on the table, he began his tale. Bea sat, totally absorbed, unaware of the tears streaming down her face as he recounted his marriage, his wife's departure, her family's demands and his fears for Liv. As he spewed the poison that had festered within his heart for the past years, Aaron too broke down, unable to continue past the point where they had met the Lady on the beach. Bea knew that part of the story, anyhow, and needed no further explanations.

Seeing him hide his face in his hands, hunched over to his knees in embarrassment at this indecorous show of male emotion, Bea's heart broke once again, but in a different way to earlier. She couldn't bear to see the man she loved in this state, and rose slowly from her chair, coming to kneel in the small space before him.

"Aaron," she whispered lightly, rubbing his shoulder gently, "I'm here, let me help you. We can make a plan."

"A plan?" he lifted his swollen, bloodshot eyes which were a perfect match for Bea's own, his tone almost scornful, so that Bea stopped touching him and rested back on her heels. "The only plan is to flee again, Beatrix. I only meant to call in and say goodbye, for I couldn't bear to leave without seeing you one last time!" The admission caused them both to begin weeping again. Seeing her distress, Aaron stood, pulling Bea to her feet with him. Taking her in his arms for the first time, he pulled her into a close embrace and cupped the back of Bea's head to his chest, resting his chin atop her.

Bea let her body be cushioned against his firm torso, the wool of his jumper itching her cheek as her tears flowed unhindered. She knew only one thing – she could not let him leave like this. She wrapped her arms around him, all thought of what was proper gone along with the notion that he could ever be hers. She knew they had no future together, wherever he may end up, given that he was already married, so she held him tightly, savouring their one and only embrace, trying to capture the feel and smell of him to be imprinted in her memory for all her lonely days to come.

NINE

As the minutes passed, and neither wished to move, it was Aaron who eventually stepped back, but only ever so slightly, so that he could lift Bea's chin with his finger and look into her eyes. "I love you, Bea," he declared, "with my whole heart, and have done since the first time I had occasion to talk with you properly." He cupped her cheek in his hand and ran his thumb over her smooth skin.

"And I love you, my darling Aaron," she responded, needing no time to consider the truth of it, and allowing herself to touch his face in return.

When his thumb trailed lightly across her bottom lip, and Aaron's eyes burned the same path, Bea felt her face raising of its own accord to meet his. At the first touch of their mouths against one another, the butterflies that had been drowned by her sorrow fluttered to life, and Bea returned his gentle friction with a sweet kiss of her own. It was so soft, and on the one hand felt so brazenly intimate, whilst on the other it felt like coming home. Bea pulled back abruptly, as her senses whirled and she was suddenly lightheaded. She felt Aaron catch her under the elbow and guide her back to the chair, where he knelt in front of her, a worried expression on his face.

"I'm well, really," she tried to reassure him. "It has simply been a day of extremes, and I am tired now. Please do not wake Liv and take her out into the night. Stay here, where you're both safe, and we can make a plan for your departure in the morning."

Aaron seemed to deliberate his options for only a second, and consideration for his daughter's welfare won out, as it always would. "Very well, my love, you go now and lie down beside Livvy and I will take my rest here by the fire."

Bea doubted that either of them would get much sleep, but she accepted his small kiss to her forehead and trudged to her bedroom, closing the door lightly behind her so as not to wake the child. She did not know if she had the strength to face tomorrow, yet face it she must.

When Bea arose the next morning before sunrise, and snook out of bed to leave Liv to sleep longer, she found Aaron already sitting at the small kitchen table, a cup of tea in hand.

"I hope I did not wake you," he smiled at her sadly.

"Not at all, I have merely dozed all night," Bea whispered back, thanking him as he handed her a full cup. She tried ineffectually to pin her hair back, but at least half had escaped from her usual neat bun, and hung in ringlets surrounding her face. She gave up, and lowered her hands to her drink instead.

"So," Aaron cleared his throat, paused, and tried again, "So, this morning Liv and I must depart in haste." His shaking hands and stammered words belied their firm tone.

"Let us just think on it a moment, please," Bea looked up at him imploringly, having had time to go through all eventualities in her head during the long, silent hours. "What if she came for another purpose. This Lady Harris. You say she has not found you in seven years, then to suddenly arrive here now… do you not find that odd? Even a little? I certainly do. Perhaps she has come for some reason other than taking Liv."

"Like what?"

"I confess, I do not know. However, no court in the land would surely give a child to a relative who is strange to them, when they have been living happily with their father their whole life!"

"As I said, she has friends in very high places."

Bea sighed audibly. She knew he was not prepared to take the risk of remaining, and decided to hold her tongue against further argument. It would be a futile endeavour and would only cause them both further upset.

"Bea," Aaron reached out in the silence that ensued and took her hand, holding it gently in his palm and tracing a pattern there with the index finger from his other hand, "my love, believe me when I say that I wish nothing more than to stay here with you. It's simply not…"

"I know," Bea whispered back, tears filling her eyes. She knew she should remove her hand from between his, but the physical touch was such a comfort, so very badly needed, that she could not bring herself to do it.

It was Liv who interrupted the bittersweet moment, staggering sleepily out of the bedroom, rubbing her eyes and complaining that her head hurt.

"Does it sweetpea?" Aaron rose to pick up his daughter, then resumed his seat, this time with her in his lap, "Perhaps you are hungry?"

"No, Daddy, I am sad. And so is Rose!" Tears filled the girl's eyes and she snuggled into her father's chest.

"Oh, Livvy, it is okay to feel sad," Bea tried to comfort the child, who all of a sudden looked tiny in Aaron's arms, "I am sad too. But it is exciting, also, starting a new chapter." Her eyes met Aaron's over Liv's head and his grateful, sombre expression melted her heart again. She continued, as lightly as she could muster, "I was excited when I came to this town, even though I knew not a single soul! I saw it as a new beginning. And that is what you will have too, sweet."

Liv nodded her head slightly and the sobbing halted somewhat. Bea stood and busied herself making eggs for breakfast. Though it was yet very early, they needed to eat to keep up their strength for what lay ahead.

TEN

Bea took time to make herself look presentable in the small bathroom, before smoothing down her clean apron and joining Aaron and Liv in the sitting room, where they had found her small pile of new stock, waiting to be displayed in the shop, and were playing a game of Snakes and Ladders.

"I hope you do not mind," Aaron looked up from the board apologetically, "Livvy saw it and… we needed a distraction once she was dressed."

"Of course not!" Bea forced a smile and endeavoured to sound as chipper as possible. She was just walking over to join them, saying that Liv could take the game on the train with her, when there came a commotion from below stairs. Hammering on the door of the shop, fit to wake the dead. Bea looked at the old clock on the mantle. Quarter past seven. Who on earth would be coming round at this time of day. Her stomach lurched as the answer dawned as quickly as the question was formed.

"Take her into the bedroom," Aaron ordered, striding across the small space between them, Liv in his arms, and setting her down next to Bea, "I will deal with it."

"No! We will face it together!" Bea exclaimed, determined not to be left upstairs.

They left Liv in the bedroom with Rose and a book, and made their way down the narrow staircase to the shop. The hammering continued incessantly until Bea lifted the blind on the door and began to unbolt it, seeing the imposing form of Lady Harris and her two burly minders through the glass. As soon as the door was unlocked, the larger of the two men pushed his way into the shop, causing Bea to jump backwards out of his path.

Aaron, however, who was right behind her, stood his ground and refused to let the man force his way into the area between the imposing bookshelves. They stood at an impasse, until the haughty voice of Lady Harris piped up from the doorway, "Oh, do let us in,

Mr. McBain, so that we are not causing a disturbance on the street like urchins!"

Reluctantly, Aaron stood aside and the three filed in, Bea closing the door behind them and following them all to the tea nook.

Not waiting to be invited, Lady Harris took a seat in one of the armchairs there, her associates standing back, next to the shop counter. Bea came and sat opposite her, with Aaron standing beside her. She could feel his anger coming off him in waves, as they waited expectantly for Lady Harris to state her case.

"I thought I would find you here, with your mistress!" the old woman clearly took a particular glee in riling Aaron.

"Why you…!"

Bea touched Aaron's arm to silence him. Hurling insults would not make this meeting go any faster. Instead she spoke softly, "Speak your piece, Madam, this is my bookshop and you are not welcome here for any longer than is absolutely necessary to resolve this."

The older woman looked taken aback at being spoken to thus, and sucked in her cheeks before continuing, "Very well." Turning to address Aaron directly, looking him up and down slowly and taking in his dishevelled, worn appearance, Lady Harris began, "I have seen the heathen box in which you force my great granddaughter to live." She raised a finger to quiet Aaron when he was want to interrupt her, before continuing, "Though I have known for years of your location. I have had you watched, of course, on occasion, and she seemed happy enough, so I let her remain."

"You let her…!" Aaron's face was red, his voice raised, and he gripped the back of Bea's chair until his knuckles were white.

Lady Harris ploughed on, unflustered, "So, you may wonder why I am here now. Well, my granddaughter, your wife…"

"She is my wife no longer," Aaron spoke calmly now, and with composure. Bea gasped and turned her head to look up at him, hearing a similar sound come from the woman opposite.

"What do you mean? Of course you are married, you never saw her to sign divorce papers!" Lady Harris sounded flustered for the first time.

"I did not need to, Madam," Aaron took a great deal of pleasure in confirming the truth, "I had the marriage dissolved on the grounds of abandonment years ago!"

Bea smiled up at him, tears streaming now down her face. He had not led her on, he had not betrayed her feelings. He was free to love. Her heart felt fit to burst and she reached back to take his hand in hers. Their eyes met and the couple shared a sweet moment of mutual understanding.

"Well! I have never heard of such a…" Lady Harris paused, mid-babble, to compose herself. "Anyway, that matters not any longer as my Guinevere is dead." She left the sentence floating between them, as if hanging in mid-air.

Aaron looked at her, shocked, "Dead?"

"Yes, my granddaughter did not follow a savoury path and she is now passed. That is all you need to know and all I am prepared to tell you. Please let me finish!" Lady Harris' voice rose as she saw Aaron about to interrupt her once again. "As you can see, I am an old woman now, and in ill-health. It will not be long before I am to join Gwen in the afterlife. That means that the inheritance that was meant to pass to Guinevere is now Elizabeth's."

"We do not need your money or your inheritance!" Aaron almost ground the words out between clenched teeth.

"Clearly!" the older woman shot back sarcastically. "Anyhap, that is not your decision to make. The inheritance will be placed in a trust for the girl, with an allowance of two hundred guineas per annum, until she reaches her eighteenth birthday."

That was a huge amount and Bea could hardly comprehend the truth of it. She sat, open-mouthed, in the silence which ensued.

"I need only for you, as her legal guardian, to sign the paperwork, so that I can die with my affairs in order." Lady Harris motioned to the smaller of the two men who accompanied her. He produced a thick document, which he laid on the table between them, flourishing a fountain pen from his inner pocket.

Aaron stepped forward, then turned and knelt in front of Bea, facing her to whisper, "What do you think, my love?"

That he would ask her opinion warmed Bea's heart, "I think that it is Liv's inheritance and you should not deny her it," Bea replied, choosing to speak honestly.

And so it was settled, the papers signed twice, one copy for each party and the portly form of Lady Harris swept from the room like a murky shadow, taking her companions with her, and saying no more on the matter.

ELEVEN

Bea shut and locked the door behind them, sinking her back against its cold, sturdy form for support. Although bone-weary in body, she had a new lightness of spirit. She looked to Aaron, bent over the counter, his hands raking through his hair. She knew he was not happy with the situation, yet it was so much better than he could have hoped. Not having to flee and begin again with the worry of being discovered, no legal battle for guardianship of Liv. Yet the facts of the matter were still a difficult pill to swallow. His daughter would be provided for, her whole life, by the family he had come to despise.

When he looked up sideways into Bea's eyes, however, felt her arm around his back, he was reminded that he had done his best for his daughter, and perhaps now was the time to start doing what was right for himself. Spurred on by this unspoken admission, he turned and took Bea in his embrace, dipping his head to find her willing mouth. There was a different passion present now, a new hope, that had been absent the previous evening, and they both attempted to communicate their longing through that single kiss. The butterflies in Bea's stomach took flight and she wrapped her arms around his neck in unfettered love.

"Daddy, I heard the door slam," Liv spoke up from the bottom of the staircase at the back of the room.

Aaron broke away from Bea, but took her hand in his, beckoning his daughter forward. "Come here, love," he said, and Livvy ran into his embrace. They hugged then, the three of them, with Liv sandwiched in the middle, Aaron raining tiny kisses on her hair.

"Do we really have to leave, Daddy? I want to stay with Miss Bea!"

"No, sweetpea, no, we can go back to our little caravan in peace!"

Hearing him say that, Bea pulled back, under the pretense of making a cup of tea for them both. What had she hoped? That he would drop to his knee and propose there and then? That he would move in with his daughter and assuage her loneliness? Of course not! Bea silently berated her own childish naivety, as she bustled in the back of the shop.

Tea drunk, a library book chosen, and Liv's few things packed back up, the man and his daughter set out in the morning sun, leaving Bea to open her little shop for the day, feeling like her heart was leaving with them.

As today was Saturday, Bea was kept busy with customers, both for the tearoom and the bookshop. Even the little library had a constant stream of borrowers. Thus it was that she sat down late in the evening, removing her shoes on one of the cosy chairs in the nook at the back of the shop, too tired to even climb the staircase yet.

When the hammering on the door began, Bea jumped, her initial thought being that it would be Lady Harris, returned to change her mind or worse. Yet, Bea knew that realistically that was unlikely, so she rose slowly from her soft perch and made her way to the front. Lifting the blind, she was surprised to see Livvy jumping up and down excitedly.

"Come in!" Bea exclaimed, unbolting the door and

opening it for them, "I did not expect to see you so soon, but you are very welcome!" she added hastily, at Aaron's frown.

"We are sorry to bother you," he stammered, clearly nervous, "but Liv wanted to return her book. We, ah, we have read it already!"

"Oh, okay then," Bea tried to hide the confusion in her voice.

Taking the book from the girl and walking to the counter, she took her pen and wooden ruler from the heavy drawer. Feeling inside the envelope for the cardboard date chart, she felt the familiar touch of a folded message and looked up to see Aaron watching her intently, his hands smoothing his hair repeatedly in agitation.

Puzzled, Bea decided not to wait until she was alone this time, and instead curiosity got the better of her. She unfolded the tiny parcel, seeing Aaron's familiar handwriting within...

My Dearest Beatrix,

You have been my strength these past few months, but this last couple of days especially. I cannot imagine what it would be to not have you by my side throughout all of life's tribulations. Your smile, your warmth, your love, are as precious a gift to me as any I can imagine.

I know that I have nothing to offer you, by way of material wealth. That is why I left this morning, fearing you would take any proposal as a desire to occupy and assume what belongs to you. Rest assured, my love, that is not the case. It is you I want, you I need, just to share my life with you.

That being said, would you do me the greatest honour of becoming my wife? I love you, my sweet Bea, and will do so till my dying breath.

With my sincere love and affection

Your Aaron

Bea's shaking hand steadied her against the counter top, whilst the other held the precious note. Tears streamed down her cheeks from the happiness that she felt might explode out of her. Seeing her reaction, Aaron came around to join her, taking her in his arms for an all-too-brief moment, before dropping to one knee in front of her. Giggling at the sight of him, Liv came to hold Bea's hand by her side.

"Will you marry me, my sweet Bea? Will you make me the happiest man?"

"Yes! Yes, of course I will!"

They kissed then, to shrieks of embarrassment from Liv, and there was much laughter and joy all around. Bea knew that this gentle man would complete her life in a way she had not even dared to imagine, and she thanked God for him.

TWELVE

With no need to delay, the date had been set for three weeks hence, as quick as the banns could be read. The few invitations were sent by telegram, and Bea had bought some beautiful material to sew a simple wedding gown. Walking past the florist on her way home from the haberdashers where she had purchased a lovely set of lace-covered buttons, Bea popped in to see her friend Eve. She and Eve had hit it off the first Sunday service Bea had attended when she first moved to the town, sharing a love of reading and nature. Although she and Aaron had agreed to keep costs down and the ceremony simple, Bea decided to treat herself to a small bouquet and had an even bigger question to ask her friend.

"Bea!" Eve exclaimed when she saw her, "Congratulations!" She came to embrace the new bride-to-be. Shorter and curvier, Eve had to stand on tiptoes to kiss her friend on the cheek.

"Ah, I see Mrs. Glendinning has been busy again?" Bea joked, knowing instantly who would have spread the news of her engagement. Long-since retired and widowed, the woman revelled in gossip and her role as a tattletale.

"Sorry!" Eve apologised, though it was not at all her fault, and Bea was not cross, nothing could dampen her spirits these days.

"Don't be!" Bea smiled, "In fact, I've come to ask you a favour!"

"Oh really?" Eve's bespectacled eyes widened and she leant expectantly against her small counter, festooned as it was in flower stalks and cuttings.

"Indeed, you see I am in need of both a florist and... a bridesmaid!"

"Ooh!" Eve squealed her delight and hugged her friend again. "Yes, twice and thrice yes! I would love to!"

"Perfect!"

"And of course your bouquet is my wedding gift to

you!"

"Oh Eve, that is so kind, thank you!" Bea beamed at her.

They set about discussing a colour scheme and choosing blooms, when Eve tried to slip nonchalantly into the conversation, "So, is it Vicar John who will be marrying you then?" Her deep red blush gave her away, even had Bea not already guessed her friend's affection for their local clergyman. The vicar liked his parishioners to address him by his first name, which the older churchgoers found far too informal. Most insisted on referring to him as The Reverend Dawson, but he just shrugged and smiled. An easy-going, friendly chap, Bea thought her friend would be very well-suited to him.

"Yes, he certainly is, perhaps it is a chance for the two of you to talk…" Bea stopped when she saw Eve become even redder.

"Perhaps," Eve fussed with her notebook and her spectacles, making it clear the subject was closed.

Bea left with an even greater spring in her step. New buttons for her gown, fresh flowers in her bouquet, and a husband-to-be whom she loved fiercely. She couldn't wait for the big day to arrive, not least because it would mean she would become a real mother to Livvy and they would live together in her small apartment, the three of them, as one family. This pleased her greatly. *Yes,* Bea thought to herself, *I have much to be thankful for.*

A Bouquet of Blessings on Cobble Wynd

ONE

Eve hummed to herself merrily as she chose the flowers which she would use to decorate the church for the coming week. As she was using pastels for Bea's upcoming wedding, she decided to go for brighter colours, picking out some lovely crimson dahlias and the ever-popular sunflowers, balanced out with some oxeye daisies. Content with her choice, Eve was kneeling behind the counter to find some matching ribbons when she heard her doorbell tinkle to announce the arrival of a customer.

"I'll be just a moment!" Eve responded to the sound, though when she stood up but a few seconds later, the shop was empty. *How very strange!* Thought Eve, searching amongst the blooms on the counter top for her large floristry scissors. She knew she had been using them but a minute before, yet they were nowhere to be found. She searched high and low, yet saw not a hint as to their whereabouts. Looking towards the door, Eve spotted one of her dahlias laying trampled on the cobbles outside, and a sunflower just inside the doorway. Curious, she went out onto the narrow street. All was quiet, as one would expect for a Thursday morning, with only the greengrocer showing any sign of hustle and bustle. Eve bent to pick up the squashed stem, turning it in her hand thoughtfully. She could ill afford to have to replace those shears, and walked back into her tiny shop disconsolately.

The floristry had been open on Cobble Wynd for many years, but had been in Eve's care for just seven months. When the previous owner, the widowed Madame Rivage, with whom Eve had apprenticed, had decided to retire to her native France to live with her married daughter, Eve's mother had produced a small tin from the garden shed. Rusty and seized shut, they had used an old knife to prize it open and the shiny contents had spilled out over the yard. Apparently, Eve's late father had been involved in some not-quite-legal importing activities on his fishing boat, and had stashed his earnings lest the village constable became suspicious. Over the years, so the stunned Eve was told, her mother and father had used the cash sparingly for repairs to their home and for books on flora for Eve. Now her father was passed to be with the Good Lord, Eve's mother wanted to invest the money in her daughter's future. The old policeman had retired, so no-one remained to question their good fortune.

"No, Mama," Eve had resisted the generous gift, but her mother was never one to back down easily.

She had stood with her hands on her ample hips and stated, "It is done, Evangeline, I have spoken to the agent and the property is ours. You will, of course, continue to live here with me in our fisherman's cottage until you find a suitable match, and we will let the rooms above the shop for a little extra income. It is what your father wanted."

At the mention of her late dad, Eve was unable to argue further, and so it was arranged and Bountiful Blooms was born. The original name Eve had decided upon was Garden of Eden, as a play on her own name, but the more righteously-minded parishioners had declared it blasphemous and had the leader of the parish council, the blustering Mr. Sutherland, insist that Eve change her signage immediately. Hating confrontation of any kind, Eve had of course acquiesced. And so here she was, a firm favourite amongst the upper class households who enjoyed decorating their townhouses with her beautiful floral creations.

Eve couldn't continue today's work, however, until she found her scissors. Another lengthy search brought forth nothing, and she resigned herself to a trip to the hardware store to purchase a new pair. *Bother!* Eve muttered under her breath, her usual good humour evaporated for the time being. She reached under the counter for her shawl and bonnet and set out with today's meagre takings in her pocket.

Head down, hurrying as fast as she could without looking indecorous, Eve rushed up Cobble Wynd to the ironmongers, owned by the dour-faced Mr. Barnett. A gentleman who could not have been more than ten years her senior, he had an air of weariness that hid any remaining youth very well. She was shocked, therefore, when she was halted in her tracks by a collision with another body. Looking up from under the fluted trim of her hat, the apology died on Eve's lips when she saw it was the vicar. Instead, a garbled stuttering filled the air, and she was embarrassed to know it came from her own mouth!

"Well, good morning Miss Wright. I see you are in a hurry!" The small smile on the man's lips told Eve he was jesting with her and she relaxed slightly, wishing her flaming cheeks wouldn't be quite so red.

"Good Morning, Vicar John, fine day."

"It is indeed! You seem flustered, is there ought I can help you with?"

Eve was sure the man had plenty of his own duties to attend to and didn't want to bother him with her silly story of misplaced utensils, so simply shook her head, "No, thank you sir, I am well."

"Excellent, excellent," the vicar hovered as if wanting to prolong their exchange, but when Eve waited silently, uncomfortably hopping from one foot to the other, he took his leave and continued down the lane.

Bother and bother again! He must think me a halfwit! Eve remonstrated with herself as she took the last few steps to her destination.

"Good morrow, Mr. Barnett," Eve tried to summon an enthusiasm which she did not feel, simply to balance the grim face of the man behind the counter, who looked more angry than simply miserable today.

"Is it?" he barked in reply, "Well, for some maybe, but

not for me."

"Oh, I'm sorry to hear it."

"Aye well, it's not every day your own wooden ladder gets thieved from below your own nose!"

"Oh my!" Eve was genuinely shocked to hear that she had not been the only one on the street to mislay things today. "I myself had a pair of floristry shears mysteriously disappear!"

"Aye? Well, a strange day it be all round, Miss, is that what ye've come to replace?"

"Yes, please, just your thriftiest pair though, I will have to save to replace the exact set I lost." Eve decided the man's misery must be contagious, as she herself felt thoroughly defeated as she left his store after their exchange, her small, brown paper parcel tucked under her arm.

Two

John made his way down Cobble Wynd, exchanging pleasantries with shop owners and customers alike. He tried hard to calm his racing heart following his all-too-brief exchange with the delightful Miss Wright. John endeavoured to clear the image of her blushing, dimpled cheeks from his mind before he arrived at his first port of call – Mrs Glendinning. It was his personal philosophy to get the worst visit of the day out of the way first, so that the day improved considerably with its completion. It was not that he disliked the woman, of course, being the parish vicar it was his job to give the same bounteous good humour to all, but she was a woman who pushed him to the edge of his natural joy. Added to that, her tendency to try to get her neighbours into trouble with her tattling put John at a distinct unease.

Nevertheless, the majority of those he had met since taking the post at the Church of Saint John the Evangelist a year ago were wholesome and friendly, welcoming him into the small community of Lillymouth with open arms. Apparently, his predecessor, the aptly-named Reverend Churchman, had been more filled with Hellfire than Heavenly Grace. His sermons had been long, rambling and prone to ecclesiastical dogma and to berating the congregation for their sins. In private, it was no secret that the man had a problem with the strong stuff. Thus, John had been a breath of fresh air in the community, or so he was told. John, himself, saw the name of the church as a good omen as to his suitability for the post and that he was there by God's own design!

John understood well the effects of excessive alcohol consumption, coming as he did from the Eastend of London, from an alcoholic father, a downtrodden mother, a one-bedroomed hovel and being the youngest of six siblings. Indeed, John was the black sheep of the family, having chosen the life of a clergyman to that of a pickpocket or black market salesman. He had felt drawn to the calling of clergyman, as well as seeing it as his way out of the poverty of his youth. The small vicarage, which came with the position here, his first following the completion of his theological studies, was luxury in comparison to what John was used to. It was lacking merely the homely touches of a vicar's wife – a situation John intended to remedy shortly!

Pausing outside the bookshop, John stepped inside to speak to his friends Bea and Aaron. Another five minutes of peace before his first visit would be a welcome reprieve, and besides, he had ordered a book on the Psalms which Bea had told him would be ready to collect today.

"Good morning, Reverend!" Bea greeted him with a smile, as she dusted the top shelves, Aaron holding the rickety ladder for her.

"Good day, friends," John replied, the cosy atmosphere and the smell of books a joy to his senses. "I came to see if my order has arrived?"

"Indeed, indeed," Bea descended the ladder cautiously, coming to stand opposite him and behind the counter.

"You must be very excited for your upcoming nuptials," John continued, "Tell me, are you having any flowers for the occasion?" He tried, and failed, to sound nonchalant.

"Of course!" Bea chuckled, seeing him blush, "My friend, Eve Wright the florist, is kindly making my bouquet as a wedding gift as well as acting as bridesmaid on the day. And, of course, she will be decorating the church as usual. Funnily enough, she was enquiring as to whether you were conducting the service!" Bea couldn't help but try to matchmake. Aaron shot her a look which told her she was being as subtle as a brick!

"Really? Excellent, excellent," John tried to disguise the fact that he was seeking information on the object of his affections, and that he was given much hope by the fact that she was asking after him. Much hope, indeed. He took the book, thanked the couple and left quickly, feeling his cheeks burn and the sweat rising beneath his dog collar.

Mrs Glendinning stood at the door of her large townhouse, tapping her foot in evident displeasure. John sighed, plastered a smile to his face and greeted her with as much enthusiasm as he could muster. "Good morrow Madam, happy I am to see you in fine spirits."

"Was there a delay, Reverend Dawson?" her bluntness grated on John's nerves and he felt his smile slip slightly.

"Ah, the tasks of a servant of God are many and varied," he retorted, accepting her invitation to enter the spacious drawing room, where a pot of tea and two china cups and saucers were already waiting on a gilded tray.

"You look out of sorts, Vicar, quite beetroot in fact! Are you well?" The woman studied him astutely from hawk-like eyes and John shifted uncomfortably in his chair.

"Quite well, thank you, the summer heat seems to be affecting my sensibilities today." Seeing a way out, and sending a silent plea for forgiveness for the white lie he was about to tell, John continued, "But, ah, perhaps I do need to rest. Maybe just a quick visit today!"

"Oh!" The hostess seemed put out, but jumped into conversation so as to speak her piece in the little time she was being given. "Well, I heard on the Wynd today – not that I am one to gossip you understand…"

"Of course," John hid his wry smile behind his cup.

"…But I did hear from Jones the Butcher that he had his best knife taken from his shop this morning, before sunrise."

"Taken?"

"Yes, sir, swiped from beneath his nose when he went out back. Then Barnett the Ironmonger has lost a ladder…"

"Lost?"

"From out front. Swiped again!" She was getting into the flow of it now, and couldn't hide her displeasure at his interruptions. "Then of course there is Miss Wright…"

"Miss Wright?" Now John actually was interested, but tried to hide it. The last thing he needed was this woman getting wind of his affections.

"Yes, she is a simple girl, it's true, how she afforded that shop I do not…"

"Ah, in relation to the missing items, Mrs. Glendinning?" John tried to bring her back on track. He ran a finger beneath his collar, wishing he could loosen it.

"Hmm, well she has apparently lost a pair of cutting shears, though as I say she is quite the giddy, scatterbrained young woman so perhaps those are still under her nose!"

John nodded and smiled as the topic changed to who was courting whom, who was on their uppers, the woman's ideas for the church fête… Finally, he ran his hands over his thighs, stood up and took his leave, backing out slowly. Mrs. Glendinning was not perturbed, and continued talking until the vicar was well out of the door and on his way down the street, grateful for the fresh air to cleanse his spirit.

THREE

Eve was busy arranging the flowers around the pulpit. The cool shade of the church building was a welcome reprieve from the heat, and she smoothed down her best summer dress self-consciously. She hoped, as always on Saturdays when she came to perform this task, that the vicar would make an appearance, and she wanted to look her best! The whole thing should really only take an hour at most, but Eve had already managed to spin it out for an hour and a half this day. She wasn't sure how many different ways she could try the flowers in the vases, or tie the ribbons differently.

John stood in the vestry, rubbing his clammy palms on his jacket and trying to build up the courage to enter the main church and talk to Miss Wright. He had spotted her as soon as she'd entered the building, her happy singing echoing around the place. He knew she must be nearly finished for the day, and he really should be making a move now to interrupt her, but his nerves were raging in full force and all courage had taken flight. Taking a large breath, as he heard her packing up her things, John approached from the back of the nave.

"Miss," he cleared his throat as all that had come out was a squeak. It was enough, however, for the young woman to turn round, blushing lightly.

"Ah, Miss Wright, what a beautiful job you have done, as usual. I, and the churchgoers, thank you."

"You are very welcome, sir, it is my pleasure!"

"Ah, excellent, excellent."

They paused, both looking at the other discreetly, until the silence became uncomfortable.

"Well, I'll be taking my leave then…" Eve paused, hoping he would say something to continue their interaction.

"Ah, well, yes, I…" John stuttered, until, seeing she was turning away, he managed, "Would you like to stay for a cup of tea? My housekeeper, Mrs. Withers, has just baked some scones!"

"Oh," Eve was stunned, her stomach flipping like a pancake, "why yes, that would be most welcome!"

"Excellent, excellent," John led the way out of the back of the church and across the churchyard to the vicarage. It was the first time Eve had entered the small cottage and she was immediately taken by its cosy charm. Sitting in two large armchairs, they chatted over their refreshments, their initial awkwardness soon giving way to pleasant conversation. When Eve caught the vicar studying her intently over the rim of his floral cup, she pretended not to notice. Likewise, when she snook glances at him, he acted as if unaware of her perusal. All too soon, the elevenses were finished, and Eve knew it would be proper to bid him farewell.

"Thank you Reverend, for a most welcome break in my day!"

"Please, call me John!" His hand brushed hers as he took the cup and saucer from her, and Eve felt a strange electricity as their skin touched.

"Of course, thank you John," Eve repeated, feeling her face flame and her heart thudding in her chest. *Surely he must be able to hear that?* She thought, embarrassed.

They paused on the front stoop, neither wanting the visit to end.

"Ah, Miss Wright…"

"Eve, please call me Eve."

"Excellent, excellent, ah Eve, would you like to come for Sunday lunch after the service tomorrow. Mrs. Withers makes a stunning Yorkshire pudding." It came out as a garbled invitation, but Eve understood the sense of it.

"Well indeed, thank you, Vi- ah John, I would be delighted to!"

And so the date was set, and Eve practically skipped back down Cobble Wynd to her small shop, closed on Saturday afternoons, to drop off her floristry tools, before rushing home to search her wardrobe.

Nothing. Not even a pretty blouse that would be suitable for lunch with a vicar. With a very handsome vicar, at that. Eve sat on her small bed, the tears streaming down her face, until she heard her mother knocking hesitantly at the door.

"Eve, Eve dear, is something amiss?"

"No, Mama, all is well." Eve scrubbed at her eyes, annoyed when her mother came in to check on her anyway.

"Really? I think not," Edna Wright studied her daughter closely, "Did something happen at the church this morning, you were longer than usual?" Edna had a suspicion that her beautiful Eve had more than a passing attraction to the Reverend Dawson, though it had never been voiced between them.

"Well, I had tea and scones with the vicar and… well, he invited me for lunch after Sunday service!"

Edna paused to hide her shock and to choose her words wisely. It may well be, she thought, that the attraction was mutual, but nevertheless she didn't want Eve to hold any false hope.

"How lovely, well, why the tears? I imagine he is hosting a meal for all the unwed young people."

"Really? Oh, that hadn't crossed my mind." Eve tried to hide her disappointment by putting her head back in the wardrobe, under the pretence of studying her few garments which hung there.

"How about your brown dress?" Her mother ventured, pulling the simple, frayed cotton from the hanger.

"Oh no!" Eve's voice rose considerably, "That is, well, it's not very becoming, Mama!"

"Oh, you wish to look becoming?" Edna quirked a smile and noted her daughter's red cheeks. "Indeed, well then I have a piece of material I was saving for a tablecloth at Advent. It is cream and adorned with pale orange poppies. Perhaps we could make you something?"

Although she was grateful, Eve knew her mother's lack of seamstress skills were almost a match for her own. She sighed in resignation, "I don't think there's time, Mama."

"Hmm," Edna racked her brain until an idea struck her, "Isn't your friend getting married shortly? The lady from the book shop?"

"Bea? Yes."

"Well, if you're going to be her bridesmaid, then you'll need a new gown, and you told me she's sewing her own wedding dress, so she must be talented in that area…"

"Oh yes, yes, you're right Mama, how clever you are!" Eve jumped up and embraced the older woman, catching her mother off guard, "I shall set out immediately when you fetch me the material!" And so it was settled.

FOUR

Bea had finished her housekeeping chores in the shop and sent Aaron and Liv out for the afternoon with a picnic lunch. Just because she was tied to the shop during opening hours, was no reason they should miss out on the sunshine. Besides, Liv had a lot of energy to expel! As the door chimed, she looked up from the book she was reading. Although the town was busy with summer visitors, the early afternoon was normally quiet as people took their luncheon and saved their stroll for later in the afternoon, so customers at this time were scarce.

"Eve!" Bea could not contain her delight at seeing her friend, "Happy I am to see you here!" She kissed the younger woman on the cheek and they both took a seat in the tea nook at the back of the shop.

"It is lovely to see you, too," Eve began, "though I have to admit it is not purely a social visit. For I have a favour to ask of you."

"Oh, do ask, please!"

"Well, I have been invited to lunch at the vicarage tomorrow," Eve tried to contain her excitement.

"Really?" Bea hid a knowing smile.

"Yes, and well, I would like to look my best."

"Of course!"

"So, I have this beautiful cotton and I was wondering if…"

"Of course, Eve, I would love to make you a dress! In fact, I have just invested in a hand-me-down sewing machine, so it should take me no time at all! Oh, it is stunning," Bea gasped as she saw the delicate cloth, "And you can wear it for my ceremony too!"

"Exactly," Eve sighed in relief, "thank you so much for understanding, Bea! I think there should be enough left over for Liv's bridesmaid gown too."

"Don't be a clothhead, of course I understand!" Bea sent a knowing wink her friend's way, giggling at the flush which covered her whole face in response, "and what a lovely suggestion for Livvy!"

So it was that the next day, Eve and Edna arrived at church for the morning service, outfitted in their best finery. Bea had lent Eve a bonnet which matched the pale peach tones of her floral dress perfectly, and they had used some ivory lace leftover from her wedding gown to compliment it. Eve had often remonstrated with herself about her generous figure, but today she felt prettier than she ever had before. Indeed, she had caught the attention of many of the townsfolk and compliments abounded in her direction, making Eve's mother fuss about her like a proud peahen!

Stepping onto the pulpit to address the waiting congregation, the vicar took the opportunity of the first hymn to study the crowd, hoping to find the woman he sought. When he caught sight of her, John was momentarily stunned into silence by the sight of Eve, sitting three rows back on a pew to the right, her face beaming as if the light of Christ himself shone down on her through the stained glass windows. Realising he had lost track of the song, John stumbled on the words until he found which verse they were up to, trying to hide his adoration for Eve by scanning his parishioners and smiling at all who caught his eye so he did not look to be singling anyone out.

The service was shorter than usual, and John knew it would be commented on, but he did not care. He used the excuse of the beautiful weather to release them all early, and stood impatiently shaking hands and muttering platitudes as everyone filed out. He noticed that Mrs. Wright left with friends, but not Eve, so he hoped she was waiting in the church for him. John need not have worried, however, as Eve was indeed sat where he had left her at the end of the final prayer, her head bowed and her bonnet resting on her brown curls.

"Ahem," John cleared his throat to alert her to his presence, "Good day Miss Wright, ah, Eve. I must say you are looking particularly charming today!"

"Thank you, kind sir!" Eve tried to convey her feelings in the wide smile with which she graced the man, and then regretted maybe being too forward. She stood, wringing her hands, but need not have worried as his own face was set in a happy smile in return.

"Let us retire to the vicarage, then," John placed her hand on his arm and led Eve out of the back of the church and across to his home. "Mrs. Withers will have returned to her family, but she always leaves the meal in the oven for me," John realised he was prattling on, but he needed a distraction from the beautiful woman on his arm.

"I'm sure it will be lovely. I have heard she is a great cook," Eve felt the pressure of his hand on the arm which was looped through his and felt the fluttering in her stomach reignite full force. "So, are any others joining us?" She tried to sound nonchalant.

"Others, ah, no, I should have thought of a chaperone, my apologies, I can…"

"No, no, just the two of us is fine!" Eve squeezed his arm to emphasize her point.

Entering the vicarage and closing the door behind them, John turned to Eve, finding himself suddenly rooted to the spot as he watched her untie her bonnet ribbons and remove the hat, letting her loose curls tumble freely. Normally her hair was tied up, so this was the first time he had seen her like this and it only served to heat his ardour further. Without thinking, John moved closer, their eyes locked together and neither wished to look away and break the moment.

"Eve, I must declare, I think you are by far the most beautiful creature I have ever seen," John looked from her eyes to her rosy lips, then back to her eyes again, standing much closer than was polite.

"Thank you," Eve whispered, her heart hammering and her cheeks aflame. She stood as still as a statue as he reached out a hand and traced the line of her face from temple to chin, and held her breath when she thought he might kiss her.

John knew what he was doing was breaking all kinds of societal and moral codes, especially since he was a man of God. However, he consoled his conscience with the knowledge that he was not leading her on. He had one intention, and one intention only – to marry this beautiful woman as soon as she would allow. His head told him to pull away, but his heart… well, his heart needed to feel her closer, to taste her sweet lips and to declare his love so that there could be no misunderstanding.

Five

Eve looked into the warm eyes of the man she had admired from afar since he first came to Lillymouth the year before. She saw now that, far from being a plain brown, they were a mixture of green and hazel, so becoming, they were his best feature she thought. As his lips descended on hers, Eve felt that her legs might truly give way under her, and clutched the coat stand for support.

Seeing her wobble, John took Eve in his arms and brushed his mouth against hers gently, feeling her release the breath she had been holding. He exerted only a small amount of pressure against her lips, and felt her respond in kind. She smelt of lavender soap and he found it intoxicating. So sweet, so tantalizing, he wanted to deepen the kiss but didn't wish to scare the delightful woman in his arms, so he reluctantly pulled away.

"Right then, let's see about this roast dinner, shall we?" John walked into the kitchen to put some distance between them, but his ardent feelings accompanied him. Turning to see Eve, her face flushed from his kiss, hovering where he had left her, he returned and took her by the hand, leading her into the room with him. He couldn't resist giving her another quick peck on the cheek – there was something about this woman that he found irresistible, and John felt like he'd just taken the lid off Pandora's box! His emotions, so long held in strict check, were now apparently footloose and fancy free. He knew he needed to be careful until she was properly his to love!

They ate in companiable conversation, the shared looks and smiles the only hint to their earlier intimacy. But when the meal was over and they retired to the parlour for a cup of tea, John found himself unable to hold back any longer.

"I know this may seem somewhat swift," he began, hurriedly, before his nerves got the better of him, "but I was wondering if you have feelings. I mean, I have feelings. Strong feelings. Ah, for you."

Eve couldn't quite believe her ears. The words that she

had dreamt John saying had actually just come from his lips, had they not?

"Feelings, yes, indeed." She replied hesitantly, "I have them too. Strong feelings. Of ah, the amorous persuasion."

"Excellent, excellent," John came to kneel before the wing-backed chair in which Eve now sat, his face solemn and earnest. "In that case, Miss Wright, I would be grateful, so very grateful, if you would do me the honour of becoming my wife and letting me love you till my dying day and beyond."

Eve felt her head spin at the monumental nature of the question, though she needed no time to formulate a response.

"Yes!" she cried, "Yes, indeed, I would love nothing more than to be your wife!"

And with that John stood and took her in his arms once again, more sure of himself now that they were officially affianced, and kissed Eve with a passion that took her breath away. She let herself run her hands over his back and through his hair before pulling away, lest all sense be lost to lustful preoccupations.

"I think we should be married in, ah, haste," John

whispered against her ear, dotting kisses along Eve's jawline which made her want to moan out loud.

"A fine idea," she whispered back, running a finger along his cheekbone and tracing the seam of his lips. "Perhaps we should let Bea and Aaron have their moment and then we can announce our engagement and be married within the month."

"Excellent, excellent, I will see about getting you a ring, my love. We have no such family heirlooms I'm afraid," A cloud suddenly marred his previously happy features, but John quickly shook it off, "So, I will enjoy choosing one for you! A ruby perhaps to match your beautiful lips," he said, honing in on her sweet mouth once again.

Eve felt like she was floating on clouds of joy. That he had called her 'my love,' was a memory Eve knew she would treasure forever. "I will look forward to receiving it," she whispered, "but perhaps we should keep our union a secret until the upcoming nuptials are complete."

"Indeed, how thoughtful and sensitive you are," John gushed, "You will make the prefect vicar's wife!"

Eve basked in his words and willed the next month to pass in the blink of an eye. She knew it would likely be the longest few weeks of her life to date!

SIX

Monday morning dawned sunny and fair, and Eve was at the shop before dawn to take receipt of the week's blooms. The town, two villages across the moor, had a market with a beautiful flower stall, and Eve shared the same supplier, she being their first drop off before they headed over there. Yawning and tidying her hair which had escaped in her morning haste, Eve was stood inside her small shop window, deciding how she would decorate it, when she was shocked to see John rush past with great urgency. He looked dishevelled, not at all his usual well-turned-out self, and had his head down as he hurried.

"Vicar!" Eve ran out of the shop, keen to steal a few moments together before the day really began and they had to pretend to be simple acquaintances once more.

The man stopped and turned, but the expression on his face was one of clear disgust as he looked Eve up and down. He started walking back towards her, then seemed to think better of it and said nothing, before turning and carrying on the way he was going.

"Well, I never," Eve clutched her hands to her chest and retreated back inside her shop, locking the door and sitting on the small stool behind the counter. Her head could not make sense of what had just happened. It was John, to be sure, in his vicar's garb, though looking dirty as if he had just climbed through a hedge backwards. But his eyes. His eyes had held no warmth whatsoever. Quite the opposite, in fact. Eve decided that there was naught else for it, he must have had second thoughts about their betrothal. She sank her head into her hands and wept.

Pulling herself together a short while later and knowing that she must open for the day, as Monday mornings were one of her busiest times with the housekeepers of the wealthier homes coming for their centrepieces, Eve sighed in resignation. Presumably, he would come and talk to her, to let her down, once whatever pressing task was dealt with, so Eve decided she would harden her heart between now and then to guard it from further pain. *Who am I jesting?* She asked herself, *for it is already broken into many sharp pieces.*

Eve was disheartened to see that her first customer was none other than Mrs. Glendinning – she really could not abide the woman, today of all days – yet she plastered a smile on her tear-stained face and waited behind the counter as her customer picked through the flowers on display, tut tutting as if they all failed to measure up.

Finally approaching the till, Mrs. Glendinning dispensed with any pleasantries and went straight into the day's news. "Did you hear, Evangeline, that Farmer Briggs at Bayview Farm has had some of his flock stolen overnight? And chickens too, would you believe it? Along with tools and such!" Before Eve could make comment, the woman continued, "And the Braithwaites, in the end townhouse, were broken into as they slept – can you even imagine it? Strangers, in your home, when you are asleep in your bed, it doesn't even bear thinking about!"

"No, indeed," Eve had enough of her own troubles on her mind, so that she was only half listening to the animated customer.

"Who could it be I wonder? No one local, I can tell you!" Mrs Glendinning paused for effect, tapping her foot on the wooden floor and clearly annoyed that she did not have Eve's full attention.

At that moment, the door opened and Bea entered. "Saved by the bell!" Eve muttered, too low for the older woman to hear.

Taking one look at Eve's blotchy face and swollen eyes, Bea said, "Good morrow ladies! I trust that all is well Mrs Glendinning?" Without waiting for an answer she continued, "I'm sure Miss Wright needs to get on, have you settled up yet?"

"Well, I..."

"Thank you!" Eve held out her hand for payment and the older woman dropped some coins on her palm before exclaiming "How rude!" in Bea's direction and flouncing out of the shop, her flowers thrown over her arm haphazardly. Bea quickly turned the door sign to closed and pulled the bolt across, before turning to her friend and saying, "How about a cup of tea and a natter?"

Eve was torn. She knew that she had promised to keep her engagement a secret, especially from Bea, whose thunder she had no intention of stealing. Goodness, she hadn't even told her own mother. Yet how could she explain her distress caused by the incident this morning without referencing it? It was certainly a conundrum and Eve bought some time by enquiring as to how Bea's wedding arrangements were coming along.

Bea could tell that Eve was avoiding a discussion on the cause of her weeping, so she chose to be blunter than usual, "Something, or someone, has upset you, dear Eve. Pray do talk to me about it, perhaps it will lighten your spirit to share the matter."

Her friend's kindness brought tears to Eve's eyes once more, and she sat her cup down in the saucer with shaking hands. "Very well, but it is yet a secret and I hope you will not think ill of me for talking of engagement when you are not yet married. This time is for you and Aaron to celebrate."

"Of course!" Bea then listened intently, shocked at the description of the vicar from the morning and how much it deviated from his normal self. She congratulated Eve heartily on her betrothal, and cautioned her against drawing assumptions until she had spoken to her beau in person. Eve was comforted by the wise words and accepted Bea's invitation to supper that evening, before bidding her farewell and opening the shop once more. It was going to be a long day.

SEVEN

Maude Glendinning paused outside her home to retrieve the heavy key from her pocket. She juggled her flowers and groceries and let slip a small curse as the bouquet tumbled back down her front steps to the street below. Seeing the familiar dog collar of the vicar approaching, she called down the street for him to come to her aid.

"Reverend Dawson, a little help if you please!" The man looked up, but did not slow his path. He had a sack slung over his shoulder which rattled as he approached quickly. Assessing that he was about to ignore her and carry on by, Maude decided she'd suffered enough rudeness for one day, and leaving the now-open front door, she threw her groceries inside and ran down the steps, standing in his path and blocking it with her ample frame just as the good man was about to pass. He mumbled something unclear, to which Maude stood her ground. He was here to serve the community, was he not?

The man looked left and right, forward and behind. Seeing all was clear, he hoisted a shrieking Mrs. Glendinning onto his shoulder like a sack of potatoes and carried her into the house, throwing her down carelessly in the parlour and causing her head to bang on the low mahogany centre table. The old woman passed out immediately and a rivulet of blood ran slowly down her scalp.

A while later Vicar John was passing the row of townhouses, their red bricks aglow in the late afternoon sun. Chatting with his friend, Doctor Allen, John stopped short when he saw the door to Mrs. Glendinning's home sitting wide open. This was unusual indeed, for she was not a woman to allow visitors to enter her home unannounced – a stickler for propriety, he knew that she would not knowingly have left her entryway free to access.

"Mrs. Glendinning?" The two men called out as they entered the property cautiously. They certainly didn't want to attract the woman's ire by surprising her.

When no response came, they pushed open the first door on the right, shocked to find the prostrate body of Mrs. Glendinning laying before them.

"Quick!" the doctor exclaimed, kneeling down to feel for a pulse, "fetch the constable!" The fine china and silver cabinets, standing open and emptied of their contents, were a sure sign that this was no accident. There was foul play afoot, and it was the local constabulary who would be charged with discovering the culprit.

"Is she dead?" John asked, hovering over the pair.

Just then Maude Glendinning came around, roused by the smelling salts which the doctor was holding under her nose, "Ack!" she screamed, looking towards the vicar, "Get you away, foul fiend!"

"She must have a concussion and be suffering from delirium," Doctor Allen announced, as John, his face pale and shocked, left the building in search of the policeman.

"My late Albert's pocket watch, it's gone!" The woman, upon seeing that her most-prized possessions were missing, let her head fall back on the carpet in another dead faint, whilst William Allen applied pressure to her still-oozing wound and tried to make her more comfortable.

When Maude Glendinning had been safely transported to the local hospital in the next town, the three men sat together in her best parlour to discuss the incident. Police Constable Hartigan said that he was following several lines of inquiry into the recent burglaries, but as yet all were drawing a blank. This being the first incident to involve brutality and bodily harm, though, he assured the vicar and local doctor that it would now be a top priority and he would be given more manpower to investigate. Cases like this were rare in their quiet town, surrounded as it was on one side by the coast and on the other by the moors.

Looking to John in particular, he added, "Ah, this is rather unfortunate, Vicar, but I do need to ask your own whereabouts at the times in question, as I have been given a few accounts of a man matching your description, dog collar an' all, having been in the vicinity when a couple of the crimes were committed. Witnesses can be mistaken and unreliable, of course, but you understand it is my duty to check all avenues thoroughly."

"Of course," John stammered, though his mind was racing and he desperately needed to get out into the fresh air to steady his nerves. He had a theory of his own, and it was not good. Not good at all.

EIGHT

Eve had enjoyed a lovely supper of bubble and squeak, and was making her way back to the fisherman's cottage which she shared with her mother. The summer sun was low on the horizon, the seagulls squawked overhead, and she felt much better about the incident this morning after discussing it once more with Bea. It had been early, she had still been tired, and the dim light and distance between them meant she had probably not been able to see his features clearly. Her own insecurities at thinking John might change his mind had come to the fore and she had likely imagined his hateful expression. Comforted when Bea had even offered to ask Aaron to speak with the man, Eve had refused and said she would approach him herself on the morrow, sure now that it had simply been her own imagination taking a flight of fancy.

Deep in her own thoughts, Eve crossed the ancient stone bridge over the Lillywater river which ran through the town, and rounded the corner of her own deserted street, where her cottage was the second on the small row of fishermen's homes. Stopping short, she came face to face with John himself. Except it was not John. It was his likeness, but not him. His clothes, but not his body, she was sure of it.

"Who are you?" Eve whispered, a feeling of fear unfurling deep in her gut as she looked into the cold, calculating eyes of the man opposite, so different from the warm face of her fiancé.

"You're comin' wi' me!" The strong cockney accent caught her by surprise, though not so much as the man's strong arm, which came around her waist so as to drag her back in the direction Eve had just come. They hurried along, Eve struggling and screaming, "Halt yer box o' toys!" he growled in her ear, the stench of him so close making Eve gag.

"My what?" Not that she cared what he'd said, really, but Eve tried to stall the stranger, en route as he appeared to be to the harbour.

"Box o' toys, noise! You with yer nose in the air, lookin' down on the likes o' me! Well, I'll show yer!" he ran faster then, lifting her off the ground completely and gathering pace as he whispered in Eve's ear the things he looked forward to doing to her once they reached his boat.

"You beast! You evil, depraved animal!" His disgusting words caused Eve to struggle harder and scream louder, so that the man stopped to fetch a filthy rag from his pocket which he shoved in her mouth before continuing apace.

Having taken a long walk along the seafront and riverbank to clear his head enough to think clearly, John was stunned to see a figure hurrying towards him in the twilight, the struggling shape of a woman slung over his shoulder. Peering closer, he realised that his worst fears were indeed true.

"Unhand her!" he shouted as he came face to face with the man, "Unhand her Jimmy, now!"

The twin brothers stood facing each other in the light of a flickering streetlamp. The sneer on Jimmy's face unmistakable as he dropped the sobbing Eve onto the stony ground and stood, arms folded, in a seemingly mocking stance. She shuffled over and wrapped her arms around John's legs, burying her face against his trousers after wrenching the rag from her mouth.

"Sure you dinna want me?" The filthier of the two men aimed down at Eve, "I'm a much better lover than 'e is!"

"Hold your tongue!" John shouted, his anger unrestrained now, as he faced his brother with clenched fists, his face red and his breathing fast. "You will accompany me to the constable with that swag now, Jimmy. Whatever possessed you to come here? What has it been? Five years? Last I heard you were incarcerated at his Majesty's pleasure!"

"Oh, get off yor 'igh 'orse John, we both know I'm not goin' anywhere wi' you!" Both men stood ready to fight, and the situation was clearly going to come to blows. John lifted Eve carefully to her feet and set her to the side on the muddy grass verge, before facing his twin once more.

The first punch landed on John's cheek and he staggered backwards, holding his face. He had never been a match for any of his siblings in a fight, and he knew well that he would lose now too, but what option was there? Eve shrieked at the impact and ran to him, just as Jimmy picked up his illicit haul and made to move past them.

"Halt!" the shouted warning and the sound of a police whistle alerted them to the torches shining ahead, coming up from the harbour. As two local constables approached, Jimmy tried to run, but John managed to yank him backwards by his heavy load, causing the man to overbalance and fall on his behind. It was enough to stall him until the policemen arrived and apprehended him, taking a foul-mouthed Jimmy away briskly to be processed once John had given a brief explanation as to his brother's identity.

Eve rushed into the arms of the sweet man she loved, cradling his bruised cheek with her palm and weeping salty tears onto his waistcoat. "I was so afraid, and I, I thought you had changed your mind," she sobbed, explaining what she had seen that morning.

"Never, my love, never," John held her close, not caring who might see their embrace. It was only fishermen returning to harbour at this time of day anyway. Besides, he wanted to shout his love for this woman to the rooftops, propriety be damned! "When I saw you there, with him, my heart was in my mouth," he whispered against Eve's cheek as he stroked her back and hair, trying to calm her. "If I hadn't happened to be passing, it doesn't even bear thinking about. If he had hurt even a hair on your head, I'd…" John struggled to calm his raging emotions given the adrenaline that was still coursing through him. "You are the only one for me, please don't ever doubt my love again!"

"I won't John, not ever," and Eve reached her face up to his and sought his kiss, needing the comfort and reassurance that she knew the physical contact would give. Her love did not refuse her, and their lips met in a passionate communion of mutual longing.

NINE

The pair made their way back slowly to Eve's cottage, holding hands outlandishly, then stood on the front stoop, neither wishing to part. Eve sought reassurance in his words and his strong arms, and John was eager to provide it, and to satisfy his mind that she was safe and well. When the night chill settled on them and both began shaking in delayed shock, John began taking his leave, albeit reluctantly. Just as he started to speak, however, the door opened and Edna Wright stood in the dim lamplight from the front room, her hands on her hips and her head cocked to one side in question. Seeing her daughter covered in mud, her skirt torn at the hem and her bonnet missing, however, along with the vicar's swollen and bloody face, she ushered them quickly inside, fussing like a mother hen.

"Well I be, whatever has befallen the pair of you?" Edna asked worriedly, fetching a bowl of warm water and a washcloth from the kitchen.

At her mother's gentle ministrations, Eve began weeping again, and John laid his arm around her shoulder. Neither had the energy to give her the full sordid account, so they recounted merely the briefest outline of the evening's events, enough to satisfy the woman's need for answers. When they were cleaned up and settled on the settee, John asked Edna's permission for her daughter's hand in marriage, and it was the older woman's turn to weep – tears of happiness this time. Knowing they were engaged to be wed seemed to put a different spin on things, and Edna soon excused herself to settle down for the night, leaving the two lovebirds together in the front room.

"Are you sure that you are well?" John's concerned gaze was a tonic for Eve's shaken sensibilities.

"Thank you, love, I am. Or rather, I will be by the morrow, I'm sure," she ran her fingers through his hair and delicately across his sore cheek, "I worry you may still have a bruise for the wedding."

"Tis no matter, it is Bea and Aaron's day and I will fade into the background, as it should be!" John looked deeply into his fiancée's eyes. Sitting as they were next to each other, but facing one another, their faces were so close that he could feel her breath against his chin. He could tell when her heart quickened and her pupils grew more dilated as he began stroking his love's shoulders and arms, before leaning in for a kiss. Their love was a hungry one now, and passion ignited in a way that neither had experienced before. Their mouths locked intimately and their hands explored faces and hair, but never ventured below the neck, both keen to save themselves for their wedding night.

"Our union cannot come soon enough, pet," John whispered against her mouth between kisses, and Eve heartily agreed. Her body felt like it was aflame and she knew she should break from the embrace, but her lips seemed to have a mind of their own.

"Aye, for I cannot wait to become your wife," she blushed further as she admitted, "heart, soul, and ah, body."

At her words, John pulled away, albeit reluctantly, as he knew that if he were to explore their physical attraction further, then they may well regret it come the morning.

"I'm sorry," he whispered, still holding her close, "I mean, I'm not sorry at all, for that was beyond wonderful, it's just that I want, ah more, I mean I need you, ah more, that is to say, it's best we stop…for now."

Eve's heart felt fit to burst with her love for this considerate, God fearing man, "Of course, quite right, though I too am looking forward to our, ah, nuptials," she hid her face in his neck at the admission.

"Excellent, excellent," John stood slowly, smoothing down his waistcoat and making a show of checking his pocket watch, "Tis late, my dear, I should be getting on my way."

And with a brief peck on the cheek, he was gone, leaving Eve's senses reeling as she anticipated their marriage bed.

TEN

The wedding morn dawned bright and beautiful, and Edna accompanied Eve to the florist shop at sunrise to prepare the bouquet for the bride, the flower baskets for Eve and Liv, and the boutonnieres for the gentlemen in the wedding party. Working with the pastel theme, Eve had procured some beautiful white gardenias, pink and lilac sweet peas, blush pink mignon roses, baby pink carnations and white lily of the valley. Sprigs of lavender were tied in with the pale mauve ribbons and the whole effect was glorious. The church had already been decorated with hardy orchids and delicate garden roses, ferns and flowering sage to compliment the colour scheme. Eve thought it her best work to date, and she was keen to show the bride-to-be!

When all was complete, Edna helped to carry the arrangements down to the bookshop and then left Eve to get changed with Bea and Liv, whilst she herself went home to put on her best rigout for the occasion.

"Eve!" Bea exclaimed when she arrived, "I'm a sack of nerves!"

"Ah, but I should think there's excitement in the mix, too, is there not?" Eve giggled, the atmosphere in the small apartment above the book shop infectious. Liv, who already wore her bridesmaid dress, danced and twirled, whilst the other two women fussed over the intricate details on Bea's wedding gown, cooing over the seed pearls which adorned the bodice and exclaiming at how well the flowers brought everything together. They dressed carefully, Eve attending to the row of thirty buttons which ran down Bea's back.

"You are perfectly beautiful!" Eve declared as Bea admired herself in the mirror nervously, "Every part the blushing bride!"

As the service was to take place at noon, it was ten before the hour when Farmer Briggs arrived in his horse-drawn cart, decorated with ivory bows for the occasion. Even Bessie the horse had her mane plaited and tied in a bow thanks to the farmer's wife! Having dropped the groom at the church already, it was now

Bea's turn to be escorted. She had initially been saddened to have no male relative to walk her down the aisle, but had asked Doctor Allen to do so and he had been honoured to accept the privilege.

At twelve midday on the dot, the church bells rang out for all to hear and Bea made her way slowly down the middle aisle of the church to the sound of the old organ. All eyes were on her, but she focused on Aaron who waited at the alter on this, the happiest day of her life. The cheerful whispers of the congregation reached her ears, as they commented on how appealing a bride she was and how stunning her gown. Bea thought her heart might burst! As Eve followed along behind with Liv, knowing that in a few short weeks it would be her turn, she looked up to see the handsome face of the vicar smiling down at her as she made her way slowly towards him, and felt her face flush bright red.

"Dearly Beloved, we are gathered here today to witness the marriage..." John began the holy service and all too soon it was over. The crowd cooed over the first kiss of the newlyweds and threw rose petals over them as they exited the chapel. There was a buzz of revelry as everyone made their way to the parish hall for the wedding reception. Even Mrs. Glendinning seemed in good humour, having been discharged from hospital the week before. She had clearly not managed to squash her hat over her still-bandaged head, so had improvised by pinning flowers to the bandage itself. It had attracted more than a few amused looks and titters from the younger generation!

"It will be us next!" John whispered in Eve's ear as they helped themselves to the buffet of dainty treats.

"Indeed, I can't tell you how I count down to that day!" Eve whispered back.

"Then come to lunch after service tomorrow and we will set a date!" John added, as he walked past, feigning a nonchalant air, to the table with cordials and home-made ales.

It was such a memorable day for the town of Lillymouth, that all spoke of it fondly for many months thereafter. Standing in Aaron's arms in the churchyard, taking a few breaths of fresh air, Bea admitted, "I never thought to wed, you know, I assumed I was destined to be on the shelf, a spinster for all my days!"

"A woman as beautiful and comely as you?" Aaron laughed as he nibbled her earlobe and dotted kisses along to her mouth, "Never! To allow such a thing would have been a crime!"

Love is the Best Medicine on Cobble Wynd

ONE

William Allen made his way slowly down Cobble Wynd following the wedding of his friends Aaron and Bea. He had been over the moon to give the bride away and had celebrated heartily with the townsfolk, the effects of the local ale now observable in his staggering gait and loud song. As he forgot the words of 'All Things Bright and Beautiful' and changed to 'Behold The Bridegroom' mid song, William clutched to the iron railings near his townhouse to steady himself, keen to get abed. The flickering luminaires which lined his path cast an eerie glow on the cobbles beneath, and in his inebriated state William saw ghosts and vagabonds in every shadow. He had not brought his overcoat, given as the day had been so warm, so he shivered now, chilled as much by his own imagination as by the cold.

Coming to an abrupt halt as he turned the corner onto his own street, William peered ineffectually through the gloom towards the doorway of number nine Herriot Row. He fancied that he saw something there, a sack or suchlike. Now, this was not uncommon, since his rural patients often paid for his services with goods, thus it may well have been a few pounds of vegetables sitting there, but William hesitated nonetheless. His vision swirled before him, so that he fancied there were two sacks and that they were moving towards him in the mist. William shook his head, trying to clear his sight, and for a few moments there was indeed only one lumpy form, yet it still appeared to be advancing.

"Damnit man, pull yourself together!" the doctor muttered under his breath, shocked when the form he had seen doubled in size as it unfurled fully, making it now just six inches or so shorter than William himself.

"Who goes there!" He shouted ineffectually, as no reply was returned his way.

Tempted as he was to turn back and flee, William decided to stand his ground and let the apparition, whatever it was, come to him. It was a sobering experience, to be sure, and his head began to throb with the after effects of one too many strong beverages.

As the shadowed figure approached, it morphed into the shape of a young boy, cap atop his head and his body encased in a grown man's clothes, which hung loosely about his slight form.

"Ah, thinking to rob me are you?" William asked, sure now of the ne'er do well's intent, "Sad you will be then, for all I have on me is a ha'penny and a handkerchief!"

"Of course I do not wish to rob you," the voice came back from the individual, surprisingly soft and well spoken.

"State your intent then!" William was beginning to lose his patience now, his bladder was demanding attention and he needed to lie his weary body down.

"Tis I, Will!" That they knew his name did not surprise, since the local doctor was known to all around. That they called him not only by his Christian title, but by its shortened, more familiar, form though stunned William into silence, as he racked his brain to think on who it might be in this area, during the early hours of a Sunday.

The figure approached cautiously, however there was a certain grace in the movements that William found familiar. When they spoke again, his mouth hung agape, so shocked was he.

"Tis I, Will, Georgie!"

"Georgie! By all the Saints, what are you doing about at night and with no chaperone? And so far from home?" William didn't know whether to scold or comfort, as there was clearly something very amiss here. The younger sister of his best friend from childhood, Lady Georgina Montague-Clarke, should not, nay could not, be here. She should be tucked up in bed in the family's country manor, some twelve miles north up the coast. It was, to be sure, a riddle too complex for William to untangle in his current state.

"May I come in, Will?" It was only then that his befuddled brain noticed how her teeth chattered and her body shook.

"Of course, though it is not seemly for you to be in my home at night!" he unlocked the door to allow them both entrance. The fire in the hearth left by his housekeeper, Miss Tanner, was now but glowing embers, yet the room still retained some heat.

"Really, Will, it is propriety that concerns you?" the sting in her tone was not lost on him, even in his stupor.

"I am tired, Georgina, and not without a little sauce in my system, so perhaps we will just retire for the night and discuss it in the morning." William desperately needed to use the chamber pot and collapse unconscious. He could not be dealing with any female drama or hysterics.

"Indeed, then direct me to a bedchamber and I will be out from underfoot!" The young woman snapped back, taking the cap from her head and letting her beautiful blond curls bounce free.

To William, it seemed as if an angel had just entered the small parlour and he chided himself on his foolishness. "Aye, quite so," he replied, leading the way up the spiral staircase and directing her to the room farthest from his own. "Goodnight Georgina!" he slurred as he used the wall to grope his way to his own door, having given the girl the lamp.

"Goodnight Will," it came out on a sob, but the doctor was too far in his cups to notice, and slammed his door shut behind him with his foot as he lurched into his own room.

Two

Lady Georgina sank down onto the soft mattress and let the tears flow freely for the first time that day. She had neither the energy nor the inclination to undress out of the gardener's clothes which she had stolen from the washing line outside his cottage on her father's estate well before dawn. She lay for what felt like hours, her stomach rumbling from having eaten nothing that day and from the twelve mile walk which had taken her along beaches and over rocks, so determined was she not to be discovered. When she had taken flight, Georgie had not thought to bring provisions, so desperate was she of the need to escape before daybreak to ensure she not be spotted. She had neither coin nor food, and had indeed been desperate enough to drink from the river water on her arrival in Lillymouth.

Sick of tossing and turning, Georgina finally decided to venture to the kitchen below and seek out some food or at least a glass of water. If Will had not been so… indisposed, she knew he would have made sure she was well tended to before retiring for the night. As it was… well, no matter, perhaps it was just as well, as it postponed the inquisition that she knew would come in the morning, for Will would know she did not come here with her father's permission.

Will awoke to a noise below stairs. The room was still shrouded in darkness, so he knew it could not yet be Miss Tanner, who did not come on Sundays in any case. His mouth felt like sawdust and his head had a volley of cannon fire within that would not cease – indeed it seemed to be aggravated by even the slightest movement. Not since he had graduated from medical college had William imbibed so much in one day, and he knew well that he would now pay the consequences. A shame too, as he had been having a very lovely dream about his childhood friend, Georgina. Strictly speaking, she was the sister of his friend, but since she was only a year and a half younger than her brother Thomas, she had accompanied them in their childhood play. Of course, the two boys had scolded her and tried to out-think the girl, but deep down they were both pleased of her company – what good was a game of Arthur's knights without the fair Lady Guinevere? And Georgie was fair indeed. This was not the first night that she had visited William in his dreams, and he sighed as he roused himself from his bed, wishing he was back in their childhood treehouse with her.

Descending slowly, Will heard the continued sounds of someone in his small pantry. Entering the kitchen cautiously, he saw the trouser-clad legs of an urchin, only their round behind peeking out of the walk-in food store.

"Caught you, you little thief!" William shouted, spanking the intruder once firmly on their derriere. He was rewarded with a very feminine shriek and the blazing blue eyes of Georgina, a barrel of biscuits in her arms.

"What in the name…!" She shouted, the harsh sound ricocheting through his sore head.

"Georgie? You weren't just a dream? You're real?"

"I beg your pardon? Of course I'm real, you saw me before you retired to your bed!"

Neither had the patience for this kind of encounter, and William raked his hands through his light brown hair in aggravation.

"Why are you dressed as a man, Georgie?" He had many questions, but that was the first to reach his lips.

"It is still night, Will, let's leave this till the morning, if you please!" Georgina tried to summon more grit than she actually felt.

Will took in the sight of her, looking frail and gaunt in the shadows of the kitchen which was lit only by moonlight. Finally, and rather later than he should have, the physician in him awakened and he took a step closer.

"Are you quite well, Georgina?" He asked it softly, shocked when she stepped back and flattened herself against the pantry door.

"Of course!" Georgie knew that Will would see it for the blatant lie it was, given that she stood here in a servant's garb, in his home in the wee hours, but she could not bear to begin an explanation. She felt the wetness on her face as her eyes began to leak again, and cursed everything that was emotional and feminine about herself. Praying that his residual affectation from the drink would cause her host to wish to return abed, she stood her ground, eyeing him defiantly.

Will had never been able to ignore a weeping woman. His male friends had laughed at his sensitivity, but he had argued that it was one of the things that made him a great doctor. He knew he wasn't living up to that title now, though, not even a quack would have ignored the state of the woman in front of him when they met – how could he not have seen it when he let her in last night? Well, considering he had forgotten she was there altogether, it had been a bad start all round.

He sought to make amends, "Let me prepare us some warm milk and you can lay on the chesterfield," William tried to cajole the frightened young woman before him. "I will bring you a blanket and build up the fire. Then I can sit in the chair," he spoke slowly as if to a child, though Georgina must be a woman of some twenty-four years by now.

"I do not wish to talk…"

Will interrupted her, "That is very well, my dear, we will make sure you are warm and hydrated and then you can go back up to bed. Judging by the dark circles under your eyes you have not slept well for some days." As he finished his sentence, Will happened to glance down. Where he expected to find boots, given the male attire, he saw that Georgina was only in satin slippers, the kind you would wear to a dance or ball.

These, which he presumed had started out cream, were now mudded and torn, her feet caked in dried sand and blood.

Georgina followed his eyes and saw what Will had noticed. She tried to hide one foot behind the other, but it was a futile move. Looking up into Will's face, she saw the shock which he tried to mask and the kindness which followed. It was the final straw for Georgie, and she began sobbing in earnest.

"There, there," Will moved to bring her into his embrace, but she held up a hand to prevent him getting any closer.

"I am well, really," she whispered, knowing that it was a ridiculous thing to say through her tears.

"I would beg to differ," Will began, being as worried about her mental fragility as he was her physical state, "but let us not discuss it further. There will be time enough on the morrow. For now, let me look after you." He held out his hand tentatively, without touching her at all, and after a few seconds of deliberation Georgina placed her small palm in his. Will led her into the cosy parlour rather than the more grandiose drawing room, and waited as she settled herself on the large settee.

"Very good," he smiled down at her, taking the jar of biscuits which she still clutched to her chest like a shield, and placing it on the bamboo side table. "I will get you a blanket and some milk, but while that is heating on the stove I'll light us a fire." He explained as he would to a patient whom he was going to examine. Will turned on two oil lamps and then hurried upstairs for a quilt.

Georgina rubbed her tired, wet eyes and wiped her nose on her sleeve. She knew that coming to Will was the right thing, but how she would persuade him not to tell the Earl of her whereabouts she had no idea. She would have to cross that bridge when they came to it.

Three

When Will returned with the bedspread he found Georgina dozing where he'd left her. His heart lurched at the sight of the young woman, looking so forlorn with her tear-stained face and bloody feet. He tucked the blanket around her gently, before going back into the kitchen and filling a bowl with warm water, then putting some milk in a pan on the stove to heat before returning to the room. Kneeling before the settee, Will dipped a cloth in the water and slowly removed the first of Georgina's shoes. She woke with a start at the pain it caused.

"I'm so sorry, pet," he soothed, "I was trying not to wake you, but the shoes were stuck to your feet with mud and … ah anyway, let's clean you up and you'll feel much more comfortable." Will dabbed at her bare skin as gently as he could, only pressing more when it was necessary to remove the dirt. When the first foot was done and dried, he repeated his ministrations with the second, as Georgina watched him intently.

"I have never in my life been so well cared for," she whispered, bending forwards, so that the words were said into his hair.

Will was shocked at the closeness and looked up, but she had already retreated, like a little mouse, into her nest.

"It is my pleasure," he looked Georgina directly in the eyes, "and I intend to make sure you are well before you leave here."

Finishing his task, Will stood and took the bowl back to the kitchen, along with the shoes which were straight for disposal. He returned with two cups of warm milk and some bread and butter, which Georgina eyed hungrily. Setting a tray on her lap, Will built a fire in the grate before sitting opposite with his own cup.

The food eaten, the silence stretched out uncomfortably. The mantle clock struck four and Will felt his eyelids drooping. "Come," he stood and stretched, extending his hand, "let's get you back upstairs."

Georgina, who was also half asleep, took his hand drowsily and allowed herself to be led back up the stairs. As they reached the door to her room, she held back from entering, and looked to Will with a sorrowful expression.

"What is it?" he asked, as they stood on the landing. He could barely make out her features, but could tell by the quaking of her body that she was afraid.

"I don't wish to be alone with my thoughts, tis all," Georgie whispered, the hitch in her voice melting his heart once again.

"Then I shall, ah, stay in the chair in your room," Will did not hesitate to make the offer, and the small smile with which he was rewarded was worth any discomfort. Seeing Georgina safely tucked up, he retreated to the wing backed chair, resting his head back as he heard her snuggle down and then the even rhythm of his guest's breathing.

Sunday morning was well under way when the two awoke. Not that Will had planned to make it to the Sunday service, nor did he think many would, given the previous day's celebrations. It was he who opened his eyes first, seeing Georgie still aslumber. Her blond curls were spread about the pillow in disarray and the bedspread pushed down to her waist. The baggy clothes did nothing to hide her womanly figure, so different to the girl Will had left behind when he set out for medical college. He had returned home only a few times since then, his own father having disagreed with William's choice to become a rural practitioner and not a physician on the much wealthier Harley Street. Whilst his family were not in possession of an earldom like Georgina's, they were still considerable landowners, and Will had been expected to run his father's estates, not leave to pursue his own career. He had left it to his younger brother, Joseph, to fulfil that role, and had been working in the Lilly Valley these two years past. Thus he had returned but seldom, and had rarely seen Georgina even on these occasions.

Georgie was aware of Will's gaze upon her, so kept her eyes closed a while longer, enjoying the heat of the bed. She could only imagine the state she looked, and wished she had thought to bring an outfit with her.

"Good morrow, my Lady," Will said gently, opening the drapes to let in the sunlight.

"Good Morning, Will," Georgina yawned and stretched, causing the already-bunched shirt to rise and display her bare midriff.

Will turned away immediately. Given his profession, he was well used to the human form, of course, but there was a difference between his normal patients and the beautiful woman awakening in a bed in his home. A difference of some considerable magnitude, in fact! Indeed, he had never been in the same room as a woman when she awoke. Feeling himself blushing like a schoolboy, Will mumbled his excuses and left to wash and dress for the day, hurrying from the room without a backward glance.

FOUR

Georgina hovered in her room, unsure what to wear. She stood in only the gardener's shirt, having discarded the trousers when she made use of the facilities. There was naught for it, she decided, but that she must go in search of some other clothing. Tiptoeing out onto the landing, she came face to face with a shocked Will. Hair dripping, encased in just a white cotton bath sheet around his broad waist, the two stood and appraised each other – she with bare legs below mid-thigh and he with a bare chest, to which Georgie's eyes were attracted like magnets.

"Ah," Will found his throat was scratchy and his voice came out much lower than usual, "Ah, excuse me, Madam." He rushed passed her towards his own room, then turned to face his guest once he was half hidden behind the door. "The bathroom is there," he pointed across the hallway.

"I have no clothes," Georgina stated matter-of-factly.

"Clothes?" Will squeaked.

"Indeed, I arrived only with what was on me!" She was starting to fret at his lack of understanding. Was the man still suffering the aftereffects of his lack of sobriety?

"Ah, then wash and I will sort something!" Will disappeared swiftly and closed the door, standing with his bare back pressed to it and breathing heavily. *Think, man, think!* His brain seemed unable to process the question of where to find suitable attire, assailed as it was by images of Georgina's shapely legs. Will took several deep breaths in an attempt to calm his raging body. He knew that, it being the Day of Rest, there would be no chance of catching the seamstress at work. His friends, Bea and Aaron, just wed, were away on their bridal tour to Scarborough, and little Liv was staying with Eve Wright and her mother. Ah, now Eve was an option. Indeed, she was probably fuller in figure than Georgina, but any women's garments were better than none. And the sooner he found some the better!

Dressed for the day, Will knocked apprehensively on his guest's door. It was opened to reveal Georgie clad only in a bedspread, her hair still dripping. "Good Lord!" Will could not contain his shock. "Parden me, Madam," he turned his back to the beautiful sight and took several deep breaths. Clearly, the young woman had no idea how much she affected him. Indeed, he had been unaware of the attraction himself until she had landed on his doorstep.

"Well, am I to go abroad under the guise of a bed?" Georgina asked stiffly.

"NO! Ah, indeed not. I have a friend who may be able to provide us with some suitable attire. I will seek her out immediately when the Sunday service is complete! Until then, I will lend you some britches of my own and a suitable chemise or tunic… The more you are covered the better!" Will muttered as he rushed back to his own chamber.

Some half an hour later, the pair found themselves at the small parlour table, hot tea and crumpets set out before them, though Will found he suddenly had no appetite. The daylight, coupled with his now alert senses, had caused him to notice more than he had the previous night. Much more. Though he was unsure as to how to address it with his visitor. Working in the rural community, William had seen more than his fair share of bruises on the womenfolk, attacked in their own homes by men who were supposed to love and cherish them. He always trod delicately, as these were private matters between the couple. Seeing such marks on the neck and cheek of someone he cared for dearly, in combination with how she favoured her left side, brought a bitter bile to Will's throat, which he struggled to swallow down. His hands clenched and unclenched under the overhang of the lace tablecloth and he tried, but failed, to avert his eyes from the telltale markings.

"You have enquiries, I suppose." It was Georgina who broke the silence first, her voice flat and harsh. Something died in Will at the sound of it. Where was the carefree girl of his youth? What had happened to make her take flight so completely?

"I do, of course, wish to know the cause of your arrival here." Will decided to lead into the topic carefully. "I am guessing by the state of your feet that you came along the cliffs and shoreline, and not by carriage or road?"

"I did."

"And you left in secret, judging by your attire?"

"Tis so." She spoke so quietly that Will strained to hear. He wished she would touch some of the food, but she sat upright, her eyes glassy and her body listless.

"You felt the need to flee?" Will reached out and took her small, pale hand in his. He was not her doctor, so he reasoned there was just the lack of propriety to take into consideration. Given that she had spent the night in his home, the two of them alone, that ship had long since sailed. So, he ran his thumb over her palm in what he hoped was a comforting gesture. Having only had cause to deal with the opposite gender in a professional capacity, Will was beginning to feel out of his depth.

The small touch seemed to cause a tiny flame to flicker to life within Georgina, for she turned to face him fully. "My father has made a match for me. He says that I am on the cusp of being unweddable, given my advancing years. My mother, of course, hangs on every word he says in simpering agreement. The match is…" here she paused and tears filled her eyes, "…unsuitable. So, here I am, seeking refuge."

Will knew there was more to the story, much more – the marks on her skin were testament to that, but he did not want to push too hard and scare her away, lest she flee once more, and land somewhere decidedly less safe. "I see. And the Earl, your father, will be looking for you." It was a statement rather than a question.

"When he realises my absence, yes."

"You know I cannot keep you here in secret?"

"I am aware. I will be on my way as soon as I can gather a few necessities."

"No, Georgie, no," Will leaned closer to her face, "No, sweet, I did not mean that you need to leave, just that there is a limit to how long I can wait before sending a message to your family. They could have me struck off if I am seen to behave… without due consideration to my profession. But remain here you will!" His words brooked no argument, and he was rewarded with a wry look.

"Do you think I did not consider the predicament I was putting you in?" Georgina's voice rose now. "Believe me, if I had had any other option… but it is you whom I trust, Will. It always has been…"

The words hung in the charged air between them. Both of Will's hands now encased the woman's and he rubbed her wrist gently, aware of the bruise which was spreading just above where he touched. He knew that her marks were resemblant of an attack, and one of a carnal nature, at that, and he tried hard to tamp down his anger lest it rise to the surface and overwhelm them both.

"You have some injuries, pet." He needed to say it, though it grieved him to draw attention to her pain.

"I stumbled on the rocks." The well-rehearsed words were uttered quickly and without emotion.

"Indeed. And your ribs, they seem to be bothering you on one side. Or is it your shoulder?"

"Tis well, I am simply tired after my journey."

"Indeed. I have a friend, a colleague in the area – Mrs. Charlton, the nurse-midwife – we will seek her out on the morrow, and she can help you with your ah…aches."

Thinking that she may well be long gone by then, Georgina nodded wordlessly, appeasing her host.

"Very well." Will stood and checked his pocket watch. The service will be over, as we slept late into the morn. Let us take a stroll to the Wright's cottage on Fisher Row and find you some suitable attire, then perhaps we will catch the sea air to help with your constitution.

FIVE

Georgina had her hair pinned under the cap which she had brought the previous night, and wore an overcoat of Will's which swamped her slight figure. To anyone giving a passing glance, however, it looked to all intents and purposes like two men taking a Sunday stroll. She had borrowed a pair of his boots, too, which she wore with three pairs of men's stockings to keep them from slipping off entirely. Her feet were so sore, that Georgina had to swallow down her gasps of pain, thus their walk was spent in silence.

Will knew he was frowning. His head still ached, but more from the current predicament than from his over-imbibing yesterday. He had no idea what they would tell the Wrights, given Georgie's strange appearance. He had lent her a neckerchief, which she had wound around the bruises on her neck, so only her swollen cheek and black eye were visible. Not that he was ashamed to be seen with her, completely the opposite in fact, but Will didn't want to start a chain of tattletaling that would spread round the town like wildfire, given the right catalyst. Edna Wright was not of that nature though, he knew, so they could be safe taking her into their confidence – though he intended to only share the bare bones of the matter.

"Good Morrow, Doctor," Edna opened the door, her best church bonnet still atop her grey curls. "What a lovely surprise!" The older woman glanced at Georgie, taking in her full appearance, but made no comment.

"Blessings of the Lord's Day, Mrs. Wright," William returned, smiling at Liv who had come to take the woman's hand in the doorway. "I, ah we, have come to ask a favour, if you will!"

"Why of course, Sir, please do come in. My Eve is away having luncheon with the Vicar so there is only the two of us, I'm afraid."

Will and Georgina took the offered seat on the worn settee and he ran his hands distractedly around the brim of his hat which rested now on his knees. "Tis a strange request, to be sure," Will began awkwardly, "But…" Only then did he realise he had not even made any introductions. "Parden my lack of manners! Mrs Wright, please meet my cousin, Lady Montague-Clarke."

The two women nodded and Edna made a small curtsey in homage to the title, before sitting in a chair. Livvy read a book in the corner, her ragdoll clutched to her chest. "A request?" The older woman prompted.

"Indeed, indeed. You see, Georgina lost her suitcase en route, and now requires a couple, of, ah, ladies garments to see her over till some can be purchased or sewn."

"Lost? Oh, my child you were not the victim of highway robbers were you?" Edna asked worriedly, staring now at Georgie's bruised features.

"I , well, it was an unfortunate incident indeed," Georgie deliberately avoided a straightforward response. "Anything that is waiting for the rag man will do, madam, and I will see you are suitably reimbursed."

"Oh, my dear! We can do better than that. I am sure Eve will be happy to lend you some summer dresses. We can bring them in at the waist with a pretty ribbon or two!"

The two women disappeared into a nearby chamber and Will let out the breath he had been holding on a long sigh. Feigning interest in the child's book, he sought to distract himself from what he knew was going to be a troublesome day.

When Georgina re-emerged from the room, a fussing Edna following behind, she was the vision of loveliness. Much more like the young woman he remembered, though more taut in feature and sadder in countenance. Will stood as they entered, and smiled down on her, "Well, what a vision, you are!" he exclaimed.

"Isn't she just!" Edna agreed. "I will package up another outfit for you, Miss, and then you will be well apported for the time being."

"I cannot tell you how grateful I am, Mrs Wright," Georgie gave the shorter woman a kiss on the cheek, and sat back down with Will.

"I'm afraid we cannot stay for refreshments," Will spoke up, hearing the water being put on the stove to boil, "we must, ah, make onward arrangements."

"Of course dears," Edna handed the package to Georgie and the two took their leave, walking back to Will's townhouse via the harbour and the park to enjoy the summer sun, both deep in their own thoughts.

Six

When they had picked at a light lunch, Will encouraged Georgie to take an afternoon repose in her room. He hoped to help alleviate the black rings under her eyes, as much as to have some time alone to get his thoughts in order. As soon as the postal office opened on Monday morn, Will knew he must telegraph the Earl. No doubt, Georgina's brother – his friend, Thomas – would be out searching for her this very afternoon, and if they found Will had harboured her secretly there would be all Hell to pay. Not least, because Georgina's reputation risked being ruined in the escapade. Yet, Will was torn. He knew that he had merely touched the surface of what had traumatised the young woman enough to flee all that she knew, she had chosen him as confidant and he did not want to betray that trust. A conundrum indeed.

Placing his teacup back in the saucer, Will stood up from where he sat behind his mahogany desk, in the study which was also his consulting room. He could swear that he had heard screaming. Opening the door a crack his fears were confirmed, and the next moments saw him racing up the stairs and into Georgina's chamber, all thoughts of what was proper gone in his haste.

The young woman lay on the bed, eyes closed, a sheen of sweat over her forehead. She thrashed about and emitted a stark keening, which touched Will's very soul.

"Georgina, Georgie," he spoke from his standing position at the side of the bed, to no avail. Kneeling on the bed itself, Will followed his instincts and took the sleeping woman in his arms, eager to wake her from her nightmare without causing her further upset. He stroked her long curls back from her face and whispered words of calm and reassurance until at length Georgina opened her eyes and the tormented shrieks ceased.

"Will?" Her bleary-eyed look was questioning, not least because she woke to find herself in her host's embrace. Far from pulling away, though, she nestled closer to him, resting her head against his waistcoated chest.

"It was just a nightmare, pet," Will whispered against her temple. "It's no wonder given what you've been through these past days." In truth, he had no definite idea as to what she'd been through, but he hoped they could lance that metaphorical boil now so that the poor thing could find some peace. "Why don't you tell me what you saw in the dream."

Georgina lay silently, even when Will made them more comfortable, sitting with his back against the headboard and holding her to his side, her top half lying across his chest.

"You can trust me, love," he cajoled, the endearment slipping out without intent.

"I know," she whispered back then, looking up into his kind eyes with her own tearful ones. Where once they had been sparkling like the ocean, Will recalled, her eyes were now a dull, almost-grey, like rough seas in a storm. "Tis not an easy ask, Will."

"I know, but perhaps if you begin with your nightmare then we can trace backwards from there to the source of it." He gently wiped the trail of tears which still ran down her face, and held Georgina to him as if their lives depended upon it.

Safe in his arms, Georgie began, albeit haltingly, "It was him. In my dream."

"Your father?"

"My father? No, it was him, ah, my fiancé."

"Him being?" Will prompted, keen to put a name to the mysterious figure.

"Ah," Georgina stalled, but knew there was nothing for it but to speak the truth, "Clarence, Baron Hastings the Younger." She shuddered at the name, a reaction which was not lost on Will.

"But he is some fifteen years your senior! He is married, is he not?"

"Widowed these past two years. With two young sons for whom he seeks a new mama. He has promised my father lands and backing in parliament in return for my hand."

Will sought to disguise the almost visceral reaction he had to this news. He had never liked the man – had found him utterly distasteful in fact. In the past, when the gentlemen left the company of the ladies and went to enjoy billiards and port at any social gathering, the Baron had regaled them all with details of his latest paramours and bed sports. To say he was a man of little class was an understatement.

"And you do not agree to the match?" Will chose his words carefully, "Surely you have a say in the matter?"

Georgina laughed, not a pretty sound, rather a harsh mockery. "A say? Hardly, Will, apparently I have had plenty of time to attract my own suitor. There have been a few, to be sure, but my heart has always belonged to… another." She dropped her eyes shyly, but her meaning was clear and hung between them like a promise.

"So, you ran when the engagement was announced?" Will asked, deciding to return to her previous statement, once the feelings of turmoil and desire in his gut had settled.

"Not quite." Will waited but Georgina did not continue. He felt the woman in his arms begin to quake, and tipped her face up to his with a gentle finger under her chin.

"Georgie, what is it? Who hurt you?" He asked the question softly, being careful to keep his anger from his tone.

"Please, Will…" Georgina sobbed openly now, and he lifted her gently into his lap, where she curled up like a child against him.

Taking time to comfort the young woman, and to calm his own response to her revelations, Will stroked her back in wide circles and kissed the top of her head, her fair curls silky against his lips. Minutes passed and neither sought to break the embrace. If anything, they moved imperceptibly closer to one another until there was no air left between.

When Georgina raised her tear-stained and battered face to his, Will had no self-control left to dictate his actions. He lowered his lips to hers and kissed Georgie softly, applying just enough pressure to create a very pleasurable friction between them.

Georgie sighed against his mouth and brought her arms up to wrap around his neck. "Will," she whispered against his mouth between kisses, returning then to taste his lips once more. Hearing his name spoken thus, fuelled the passions inside him so that Will felt he was being consumed from the inside out by a raging fire. Reluctantly, he pulled away to put a small distance between their faces, taking the opportunity to gulp in some much-needed air.

"My apologies," he whispered regrettably, "I should have restrained myself."

In reply, Georgina moved to kiss him again, no longer caring if she appeared wanton. William found himself unable to refuse her and they kissed passionately once more.

SEVEN

The heat that burned between the pair and their thirst for each other was seemingly unquenchable, and Will worried that, should they continue, Georgina's virtue would be at risk. Pulling away abruptly, disgusted with himself, he silently berated the fact that she had come to him for sanctuary yet all he offered presently was seduction.

Will cleared his throat, buying time for his ardour to cool. Georgina sat up slightly, so that her small chest was no longer pressed against his torso, and glad Will was for it. It felt like there was not enough air in the room for them both, so breathless were they.

"Please do not apologise again," Georgina beat him to the remark.

"Very well, but, ah, know that it cannot happen again. You are betrothed, and we are old friends."

It was Georgie's turn to pull away now, the hurt on her face evident, such that Will felt her rejection as a physical blow.

"I am NOT betrothed," the young woman corrected forcibly, turning to face Will with the first fire in her eyes that he had seen since she'd arrived. Other than that which his kisses had put there, of course, but Will was trying to forget that! "I will not be returning to that... that..." Georgie struggled to find an accurate description for her father's match for her, and her renewed trembling told Will all he needed to know about who had assaulted her.

Needing to hear it from Georgina's own lips, though, he pursued his previous line of questioning, "Is he not kind?"

"Kind?" Georgina spat the word as though it offended her greatly, then turned on Will with a look of abject hatred. "I doubt he is capable of the sentiment! Even with his dogs!" She stood up with that and walked to the window, opening the drawn curtains to let in the late-afternoon light.

Will stood and moved to her side of the bed, waiting

just behind the young woman, so that when she turned, her pale fists clenched, they were less than a foot apart.

"Tell me, Georgie," the words came out pleadingly.

Taking two deep breaths, Georgina walked forward a couple of steps and wrapped her arms about Will's waist. Not having the heart or the desire to push her away, he held her in the same way, resting his chin atop her head.

"We went to the Summer soirée at Lord Cunningham's estate these two night's past," she began, speaking into Will's chest, "It was to be the announcement of the engagement, so my father made a grand show of the matter and all who were in attendance sought to congratulate me and…him. My fiancé would not let me leave his side all evening. In the end, under the pretence of powdering my nose, I sought refuge in the gardens for a breath of air, and to calm my growing anxiety. After an all-too-brief respite, he sought me out and found me there, beside a fountain surrounded by ornamental bushes." Will knew the area she described, having been there himself many times. He nodded to encourage her to continue and because he feared that speaking would release the anger which was barely contained within him.

"So, he alluded to the fact that I was now his to do with what he wanted, pawing at me as he did so," Georgina's voice hitched and she struggled to force back the sob that rose in her throat. "When I contradicted him, and said we were not yet wed, he mocked me and spoke of taking what he wanted whether I was willing or nay." The tears could no longer be held back, and Georgie let them flow freely against Will's waistcoat.

"And, ah, did he succeed?" Will did not wish to upset the lady further, but he needed to know the extent of her injuries, visible and invisible.

"Nay," she whispered, "Not in the totality to which you refer anyhow. My maidenhead is yet intact, though it came very close to that not being the case." She shuddered and felt the room spinning around her. Catching her in his arms as she fainted, Will laid Georgina on the bed and sat down beside her, rubbing her hands gently in an attempt to rouse her. Thankfully, she came around without him having to fetch the smelling salts from his case, as he did not want to leave her alone.

Will heaved a sigh of relief when he saw Georgina's eyes fluttering open, though the tears began again immediately. He felt anger like he had never known before flood his senses. "By God, I'll have him flogged!" he spoke aloud, when he should have kept the thought to himself. Georgina immediately sat up and shook her head vehemently.

"No, Will, please, I want no more bother. Please do not implicate yourself on my account!"

Will struggled to get a handle on his emotions. Through gritted teeth, he whispered, "Can you point to where he hurt you?"

Reluctantly, Georgina indicated her neck, her chest, ribs and wrists, and lower to her hips and abdomen. "Lucky it was, that an older couple heard my distress and came to investigate," she continued, "He tried to make out that it was a simple lover's tryst, but the fear in my eyes must have alerted the woman, for she came closer to check on me. Seeing the hand marks about my décolletage, she asked if I wished to remain with the man. His grip on my wrist increased, but I shook my head and so they kindly escorted me back to the main gathering. I feigned a malady and my father reluctantly had the carriage take me home. He was well in his cups by then so my mother accompanied me, taking to her bed the moment we arrived at the manor. I found some gardener's garb and, well, you know the rest. Though it did take me a whole day to walk here and at times I felt I would never arrive!"

"Come here, pet," Will sat against the headboard once more and lifted the weeping woman into his lap. There was no way on God's green earth he was letting her return either to that place or to that beast. A protective and possessive urge filled him, that had something to do with her predicament, but was more, he admitted to himself, the result of his own feelings for the young woman. If she would have him, he would make her his, her family be damned.

EIGHT

Georgina rested against Will once more, grateful for the safety which he offered. She tried to calm her trembling nerves and slow her breathing, willing the tears to stop. *What must he think of me? A cry-baby who cannot control her emotions!*

As if he had read her mind, Will spoke up, "Let the tears flow, love, better out than in! You have been through a terrible experience, and you need time to process it. Do not be embarrassed."

"Thank you," Georgie graced him with a watery smile and they sat quietly together, lost in their own thoughts.

At length, his mind made up, Will spoke. "My dearest Georgina," he began, his face solemn, his nerves ragged, "I wish we had longer for you to recover and for us to explore the relationship that I believe may blossom between us. However, that is not the case. Your family will be searching for you, and in a day or so, two at most, I must telegraph them that you are safe. So, I would be honoured if you would become my wife, to cherish and to protect for always."

"No, Will."

"No? I do not understand."

"I would not have you throw your life away on my account."

"Throw it away? But you have feelings for me, do you not?" Less sure of himself now, Will scraped his hair back with his hands, his heart thudding as he awaited her answer.

"Indeed, for as long as I can remember, both girl and woman have loved you. But I wish for you to marry for love."

"Oh, sweet, I do love you, of course I do, could you not tell it in my embrace? I was just a fool to not realise it sooner, thinking you were beyond my reach."

"Then I would love nothing more than to become your wife!" Georgie leant up and wrapped her arms around

Will's neck, their faces touching, and scattered small kisses about his cheeks. Will groaned aloud, encircling her waist with his strong arms and kissing the young woman passionately, until both were breathless once more.

"Ah, let us leave the lovemaking till we are wed, pet," Will whispered, "You are yet sore from your ordeal and it will be so much the sweeter knowing we are one in the eyes of God."

As the sun set outside, the pair dozed in each other's arms atop the bedsheets, the effects of the previous twenty four hours catching up with them both. Waking languidly, Georgina stretched and smoothed down her dress, looking at the man who snored lightly beside her. What she had done to deserve such a blessing, such a gentle man, Georgie did not know, but thankful she was for him.

After eating a supper of pie and potatoes, the couple sat in the parlour, their knees touching as they shared the large chesterfield, and considered their options.

"There is naught for it, but I must speak to the Reverend Dawson, and in haste," Will stated. "He will know the best course open to us. I hope he can marry us without any further delay, but I admit I do not know the rules under which he works with regard to announcing the banns and suchlike. What is clear, however, is that you must remain closeted until the ceremony is performed, we cannot have you being discovered!"

"I feel safest when I am with you, love," Georgie whispered, her lower lip trembling.

Will's head told him to leave her at home, but his heart was touched by her display. "Very well, we will hurry to the Vicarage shortly after dawn, taking the back alleys, and see what he advises."

The decision made, they shared a brief embrace before each took a cup of hot milk from the stove and retired to their respective bedrooms.

Will tossed and turned, unable to find his slumber. His thoughts flew around his head like starlings, tweeting about how he should keep Georgina safe and wed her, and deal with her father, and make everything well for her. Around and around they went, until he was feeling sick with the muddle of it. Deciding to give up on sleep, he stood and dressed casually in trousers and a shirt, then tiptoed down to his study. Taking a sheet of paper from his pad and his fountain pen, he went to sit by the unlit fire to formulate a list. The words would not come, however, as Will had no idea how to proceed other than to speak to John in the morning. They could elope, of course, North of the border, to Berwick or even Gretna, but that required a residence in Scotland of twenty-one days before the ceremony could be conducted, thus carrying a huge risk of discovery by Georgie's father, who had connections throughout the land. No, a quick ceremony here in the locality was what was needed.

Roused from his thoughts by a small cough in the doorway, Will looked up to see Georgina standing there. Her hair was tumbling about her shoulders and she wore a nightgown which Mrs Wright must have given her in the small additional bundle of garments. Such a beautiful sight was she, that Will could do naught but stare.

"Sorry I am to disturb you," she whispered, "but my dreams plagued me once more."

Looking more closely in the lamplight, Will saw the traces of tears down her face. "Come here, love," he beckoned her forward and onto his lap, where she snuggled down and soon fell asleep.

And so they stayed, the rest of the night, nodding off in each other's arms until the light of dawn filtered through the drapes.

NINE

John was not unaccustomed to being roused from his bed by parishioners, especially when there was an illness or, God forbid, a death in a local family who requested his prayerful presence. As Monday was his normal day of rest in the week, however, John was slightly perturbed to be woken by the sound of gentle tapping on his window. Knowing Mrs. Withers would not be here for a while yet to answer the door, John staggered to the front porch, pulling his robe about him as he went. Shocked he was to see the local doctor and a young lad in a cap standing there.

"Doctor Allen, ah William, is there an illness?" He asked, trying to get his sleep-filled thoughts in order.

"Ah, no, Vicar, may we come in?"

"Of course!" John remembered his manners and ushered the two into his study. "When I escorted Eve home yesterday," John paused and blushed, though it was lost on Will who stood anxiously wringing his hands, "her mother, ah Mrs Wright, mentioned that you had your cousin staying. He looked Georgina up and down, "but I was led to believe it was a female relative!"

Will looked to Georgie then back to the Vicar. "Ah, perhaps we should sit!"

When the bare bones of the matter had been conveyed to the clergyman, and he had been reassured several times that the couple were not, in fact, related, they sat in awkward silence as he processed the information. It was not the first time John had been met with the request of a quick ceremony, of course, but he had not expected it from his friend.

"Well, you know that I cannot wed any couple without either the banns being read for three Sundays in a row, or if not then a common licence is required, obtainable from the office of the Bishop's clerk."

"Indeed? So if I were to ride out and procure this, then you could perform the ceremony?" Will asked, the light of hope shining in his eyes.

Georgina, who had remained silent as the two men spoke, took his hand and squeezed it.

"Yes, though you must take someone to vouch for you, and the bond of course, which guarantees that the details you give are correct," John explained.

"I have only my bicycle that I use for my home calls," Will thought aloud. "I will need to borrow a horse, and find a safe place for Georgina to wait."

"Indeed, there is a lot to consider," the Vicar nodded sagely, torn as to whether he should offer his own services, given the man was more friend than congregational neighbour. Mind made up, he ventured, "We shall borrow horses from Farmer Briggs. We can leave Georgina with Eve, her mother and Liv, she will be perfectly safe there."

"I am indebted to you!" Will stood up to shake the man's hand, and Georgina went into the kitchen to make breakfast for them all, whilst the Vicar disappeared to dress. Plans made, there was a new spring in William's step and he took a moment to pray that God would bless their union and allow it to go ahead unhindered. Now, there was the matter of timing the telegram so that it arrived when it was too late for Georgina's father to do ought to stop the marriage. Will decided that he would telegraph the Earl upon his return with the licence, then by the time it was received and acted upon, he and Georgie would already be safely husband and wife.

TEN

Returning with the marriage licence, Will felt himself emboldened, as if coming back from battle to his waiting sweetheart. He thanked the farmer and paid him for the use of two horses which he now returned, and he and John rushed down the hill to the fisherman's cottage where the women waited. John had shared his own engagement news with Will on their journey, and both were keen to see their fiancées, though it had been but a day's separation as they travelled to the nearby city and back. On seeing Will, Georgie rushed to him and put her arms about his neck. Those assembled turned their backs to allow the couple some privacy, and Eve looked shyly at John, who smiled his love for her. Theirs was not a love suited to public displays of affection, but a shared smile conveyed all either of them needed to know.

Arrangements were made for Georgina to stay with the Wrights for another hour or so to prepare for the ceremony, borrowing a gown once again from Eve, who also kindly offered to make up a small bunch of flowers for the bride. Will, meanwhile, rushed to the postal office on Cobble Wynd before it closed for the day, whilst John returned to the vicarage to freshen up and don his robes. The doctor sent a brief telegram to Georgie's father, the Earl, stating that his daughter was safe and they were to be wed, before hurrying home to put on his Sunday suit.

As William descended the stairs, looking fine in his best attire, adjusting his cravat absentmindedly, there came a commotion out front, hammering on his door and shouting, "Doctor Allen, Come quick!" As Will's heart thudded in his chest, his first though was that it was Georgina's family. Reason soon prevailed, however, when he realised that, although her father would have the telegram by now, they could not have made it here that fast even on their speediest horses. So long as he hurried to the church to meet his bride without delay, all would be well. The question remained, though, who was at his door?

Opening it cautiously, Will was met with the panicked face of Constable Hartigan, a hunched Mrs. Hartigan on his arm, doubled-over in pain. Will could not refuse them, being as he was the only physician in the area, so he ushered them into his treatment room quickly. A brief examination told Will that his worst fears were likely correct – an acute attack of appendicitis. There was nothing for it, but that Farmer Briggs must be messaged once more, as he had the nearest horse and trap that was quickly available, and the poor woman must be taken to the cottage hospital in the nearest town. This would take time, of course, and whilst the policeman went to fetch the trap for his wife, Will tried to keep the woman comfortable, eventually giving her a sedative to calm her. All the while, of course, thinking of his bride who would be waiting at the alter for him.

Georgina stood with Eve, Mrs Wright and Liv at the pulpit, adjusting her bonnet nervously. Whilst they had at first reassured her that her affianced would surely be there at any moment, even the vicar was now starting to look concerned. Not that William would have had a change of heart, but rather that some foul deed or mishap must have befallen him en route to the church.

"I will go to look for him," John spoke up eventually, "for he must be nearby." Just as he was about to exit from the side door, however, the main doors of the church were thrown open and none other than the Earl of Newcastle stood there, his son Lord Thomas and Georgina's fiancé, Lord Clarence, flanking him on either side. They had obviously ridden hard, for all were red faced and windswept, the Earl having a look of black rage which he directed straight at his daughter.

"Georgina! To me, NOW!" He bellowed, but Georgie stood still, tears streaming down her face, clasping Eve's hand as if it were a lifeline.

The three men advanced on the small group, just as the side door also swung open and Will rushed in, equally dishevelled.

"I saw horses in the churchyard!" He shouted, before skidding to a halt, faced with Georgina's menfolk.

"What is this?" The Earl kept shouting random questions, clearly his chosen method of getting information. Little Liv screamed and shook as his voice echoed around the vaulted ceiling of the church, and she buried her head into Edna's skirts.

"Hold your tongue," John finally found his voice, so shocked had he initially been at the intrusion, "For this is the house of God!"

Will looked to Georgina, then to the vicar and back to his love. Striding across to stand beside her, he spoke directly to John without a backward glance to the men who advanced up the church aisle. "Marry us, Reverend, and be quick about it please."

"You will not!" The Earl barked, coming up behind Georgina, grabbing her arm and yanking her backwards. Her other arm was linked through Will's so she stood now, stretched between the two.

"Take your hands off my fiancée!" William ground out, looking the young woman's father directly in the eyes and not flinching.

"I think you will find she is my fiancée," Clarence spoke for the first time, his scornful gaze not without mockery as he looked William up and down."

"You, who ABUSED HER!" Will launched forward, only to find himself dragged back by John.

"There will be no blood shed in the House of God!" It was the first time any of the assembled had heard John raise his voice for any reason. Even the blustering Earl held his tongue for a moment.

"Lady Georgina," John continued, "Please tell me, in your own heart, to whom are you betrothed?"

"To Doctor William Allen," Georgie spoke without hesitation, looking directly at her love. "See Father," she turned to the Earl, "see the marks your choice of husband laid about my body as he tried to force himself upon me!" She lowered the stiff collar of her gown to expose her bruises, though her face was also still black and blue for all to see. Wrenching her arm free of her father's grasp she turned up her sleeve and showed him her marked wrist too.

The Earl showed only a brief look of shock before it was hidden again behind a mask of incredulous authority. "Yet, you remain my property! The Baron will be sternly spoken with," he turned briefly to Clarence before returning to face his daughter, "but you are mine to give to whomsoever I choose. Hell and damnation, girl, why must you embarrass me thus? You are a disobedient chit, to be sure!"

"No blasphemy here!" John was clearly angry now. He did not believe that a woman of four and twenty years should be the property of any man, not even a husband. "The young lady has clearly stated that she is affianced to the good doctor. I have the licence here, signed by the Bishop himself, and this wedding WILL proceed." He stared the Earl down in an apparent battle of wills. "You will either leave this holy chapel or bear witness to the ceremony, but you WILL NOT be taking the bride without her consent."

Eve looked up at her love adoringly, she had never seen him take charge like this, and she felt she might swoon from the feelings it evoked in her! Will and Georgina held each other close and turned their backs to her father.

"But you were my friend, Will!" Thomas finally spoke up. It was clear from his attitude towards Clarence that he did not favour the match between the man and his sister, but he had no say in the matter once his father's mind was made up. "How can you ruin my sister so?"

"Ruin me?" Georgina spat back. "To be married for love is not ruination, brother! You would do well to try it!"

"Very well, we will proceed in God's Holy name and under His watchful gaze," John began, as the Earl made a show of storming out, ruing the day he ever begat a daughter and shouting that she was to be cut off from all future inheritances…

When the chapel was quiet again, and the stillness of God descended over the place, John took a deep breath, "I think we should continue without delay, in case they return with the local magistrate," he said, and Will and Georgina were quick to agree. The ceremony itself was short, but emotional, and there was not a dry eye left when it was over. The newlyweds kissed briefly, thanked everyone heartily and set off into the night, ready to begin their married life together.

"I think a honeymoon is in order," Will whispered into his bride's ear. First thing tomorrow we will take the train south and have some time getting to know one another properly. I will buy you some new outfits on our arrival and we will act like young lovers should. No more worries, my love." And with that he paused under the ornate streetlamp to kiss his new wife.

"I love you, Will."

"And I love you, my sweet."

Epilogue

A beautiful Monday at the end of August, in the Year of our Lord nineteen hundred and ten, saw the residents of Lillymouth assembled in the church once more, this time for the marriage of the Reverend John Dawson and his beautiful bride, Eve Wright. The Bishop himself had travelled to the town to conduct the ceremony, a fact which had caused not a small amount of fuss and excitement amongst the congregation. The church was fuller than it had ever been, with everyone in their finery. From the local landowners to the farm hands, all were keen to share in the celebrations.

Eve and John, however, cared little for the exact numbers in attendance, so engrossed were they in each other. As Aaron walked the bride dawn the aisle to *Air from the Water Music* by George Frideric Handel, John stood facing the alter, waiting until Eve was beside him to turn to face her. When he did so, he was greeted with such a radiant smile from his love, that he felt his legs go weak at the knees at the sight of her. From the flowers in her hair, to her dainty bridal shoes, she was the picture of perfection!

Edna Wright sat on the front pew weeping happy tears, with Beatrix and Liv next to her. Beside them, Doctor Allen and his lovely wife, Georgina sat close to one another, sharing a mutual look of contentment. All beamed at the couple, heartily glad to see their friends married and to partake in their happiness.

"You are a vision of loveliness, my sweet," John whispered to Eve as she came alongside him.

Eve blushed, her nerves already heightened by being the centre of attention – a position she was neither accustomed to nor comfortable with.

"Thank you, John, I am the happiest of women to be wedding you!"

And so they became man and wife, to share their lives together under God's loving gaze, thankful for his bountiful Blessings.

Love is patient, love is kind. It does not envy, it does not boast, it is not proud. It does not dishonour others, it is not self-seeking, it is not easily angered, it keeps no record of wrongs. Love does not delight in evil but rejoices with the truth. It always protects, always trusts, always hopes, always perseveres. Love never fails.

1 Corinthians 13:4-8 NIV

About the Author

Anne Hutchins is a pen name of romance writer, R.A. Hutchins. She lives in the U.K. with her husband and three children and loves writing romance books, as well as researching about different points in history. In her spare time, she enjoys pottering in the garden!

Other Books in the Cobble Wynd Series

A Lesson In Love on Cobble Wynd

In 1911, fiercely independent school teacher Florence Cartwright finds herself taking up lodgings in the home of widower and local constable, Robert Hartigan. Whilst her host remains in an oblivious stupor, Florence does her best to help his three children with their own problems, putting herself in danger in the process.

When higher powers force the couple to form a relationship much closer than either of them would wish, will they be able to overcome their own frustrations and resentments, and move on to something more fulfilling for them both?

Whilst this second book in the Cobble Wynd series does feature some familiar characters from the first book, this story can certainly be read as a standalone novel.

Available to pre-order on Amazon now! Release date June 10th 2021.